ALSO BY CLAIRE AMARTI

The Silent Daughter

BOOK CLUB DISCUSSION GUIDE

To download a free Discussion Guide for this novel,
please visit claireamarti.com/welcome

THE FIRST WIFE'S SECRET

CLAIRE AMARTI

For my grandparents,
Madge and Tom Anderson, and May and Gerry
Wheeler,
In celebration of what lives on

Prologue
Lottie

The shards of broken glass are everywhere.

I'm standing in the garden in the middle of the night, with the wreckage of the party all around me. The white tablecloths have come unmoored, flapping like shrouds in the dark. There are plates on the tables with unfinished food still on them.

I sink down onto one of the rented party chairs and turn my face up to the sky. The night song of cicadas is all around me, but what I hear are the sounds from hours ago: blaring sirens, breaking glass, a scream. The noises fill every inch of my skull. I close my eyes and see the red and blue lights of an ambulance racing away from me.

Was it really just hours ago that we were all gathered to celebrate what should have been a perfect day? I stare up at the night and its indifferent stars. *Wake up, Lottie*, I tell myself. But there's no waking up. This is reality now, and there's no way out.

I close my eyes again.

How could this happen to us?

How could it catch us so off guard?

And where on earth do we go from here?

Chapter One
Dinah

Twelve hours earlier

'I still don't get it.' Max Brannagh crosses his arms and frowns at me. 'Don't you *want* me there?'

It's three in the afternoon and already sweltering. The anniversary party's going to be one sticky mess. I can picture it now, the women with makeup running down their faces, dripping off their noses; everyone drinking too fast in the heat; and Dad's poker buddies starting into their inappropriate jokes before the food's even served.

'Come on, Max,' I say. 'You'd *hate* it. You know you would.'

It's my fault my boyfriend isn't invited to our big family party. Or at least, that's what he thinks.

Max frowns back at me. And though I feel bad, I have to admit he's very handsome when he's frowning. His eyes seem to get darker, somehow, and he seems an inch taller. In his jeans and plain white T-shirt he's like a modern-day James Dean. Usually when I see him he's coming straight from work and rocking his front-of-house blazer, with sharp shoes and gel in his hair. I like him this way though—looser, more untamed. But I still have to deal with the fact that he's feeling wounded and a little mad at me. Maybe more than a little.

'I just think it would have been a nice opportunity,' he goes on. 'To spend some more time with your parents.'

'Not my parents,' I remind him. 'My dad and my stepmom.'

Max looks impatient. 'I know, Dinah. But your dad's so busy. In almost a year I've barely met the guy.'

Which is true, and it's by design. But of course, Max doesn't know that.

Dad's ridiculous, stubborn disapproval of my relationship with Max has strained things these last months. Max is under the impression that Dad's basically a workaholic, and just happens to be out of the house when Max and I 'drop in'. Unfortunately, Dad shows no sign of getting over his issues and the way things are going, I figure it's only about to get worse.

Maybe that's the reason for this feeling I've had all day, this sense of something looming over me. It won't be hurricane season until the end of summer but that's kind of what it feels like: a hot, grey shiver of unrest, rippling through the air.

Or maybe it's just that I'm dreading this damned party.

Max and I are in the park at the top of Main Street, a pretty little spot with picnic tables and a fountain. Birch Bend is a picturesque—*mostly* picturesque—

town in upstate New York, a part of the world I spent all my teenage years wanting to escape from and that I came back to three years ago with my tail between my legs. The funny thing is, I don't mind being back here any more. After the breakup with Jeff, I was done with bright lights and big cities. And Dad helped out so much with Josie, it made life easier to live nearby.

Max brushes down one of the park benches—it's already clean, but he's like that—and we sit. I look around at the picnic tables already packed with families, the groups of teenagers sneaking beers in brown paper bags. I've always liked coming here to people-watch, spying on the happy families and wondering what the secret is.

Maybe one of these days, I won't have to wonder.

'So have you thought about—' Max starts, but I put my hand over his.

'Give me a few more days, Max? Please?'

Neither of us needs to say it out loud to know what we're talking about. It makes my heart race a little when he brings it up.

His frown deepens and I go to take his hand, but as I turn my wrist I can't help glancing at my watch. Max gives me a withering look.

'I'm *sorry*,' I say. 'I'm really sorry. But—'

'But you need to go.'

'I have to find something to wear,' I say. 'And something for Josie to wear. And the house... you know what Mara's like.'

Max sighs, and pivots so we're walking back towards the park entrance. His stride is fast but I find his hand with mine and thread my fingers through it. He slows his pace just enough to let me.

'This isn't forever,' I say, and look him square in the eye. 'I promise.'

He sighs heavily, and there's the ghost of a smile.

'It better not be,' he says, and leans in to kiss my hairline. 'I don't think I could bear it.'

I look up at him, and he looks back. It's that intense, hungry look of his, not a smile but maybe better than a smile.

'So am I going to see you this week or what?' he asks.

Normally Max and I try to plan a couple of date nights a week—it depends. We only live thirty minutes apart, but getting alone time as a single mom isn't so easy. This weekend is out of the question though, since Josie and I are staying overnight at Dad and Mara's tonight, and Mara's doing a "family brunch" tomorrow. It's all part of Mara's Grand Plan for their anniversary party. My sisters and I are all staying over at the old house, each of us back in our childhood bedrooms—though since Lottie still hasn't moved out of hers, I guess she doesn't count as a guest.

'Monday?' I suggest to Max. 'I'll see if Trisha's okay to take Josie for a sleepover.'

Trisha's my neighbor in Rhodesbury, one town over, and she has a daughter Josie's age.

Rhodesbury's pretty similar to Birch Bend only less wealthy, without all the cute boutiques on Main Street to lure in Vermont-bound tourists.

'Okay,' Max says, his voice still a little taut. 'Monday then.'

We say goodbye and I watch him go, walking the way he always walks—like a spring is coiled inside him, barely held back and ready to spring.

When we were teenagers growing up in this town, Max Brannagh was more my sister Vaughan's type. I hung out with the alternative kids mostly, the musicians and the wannabe goths; Max was preppy in the same all-American way my sisters have always been. He was just another face on the football team line-up, another not-so-good good boy who held doors for teachers and yes-sirred his elders, then got wasted on the weekend and vomited in the neighbors' swimming pools.

At least that's how he seemed back then. When he talks about his high school years to me now, it sounds like he didn't go to that many parties after all. He didn't have such an easy time fitting in with the other guys, plus he always had to work at his family's restaurant in his spare time.

And then last October he came into Bud and Branch, wanting a quote for flower arrangements for the new café he'd just opened. It had been years since I'd seen him but I recognized him right off. People in Birch Bend tend to know the Brannaghs but the recognition's not always mutual. Frankly,

I'm glad to be from one of the families that keeps a lower profile. The Brannaghs are not exactly well-liked. They kind of have a tendency to lord it over other people. Max's mom Alane used to be a big deal on the PTA back in high school and she's still one of those Ladies Around Town, always cutting a ribbon on something or spearheading some local committee or other. I've never felt like there's a class divide between Max and me, but I'm sure his mom thinks so.

Max's grandfather started Brannagh's, their family-owned restaurant, which has been kind of an institution in Birch Bend for decades. Lots of my friends had summer jobs there over the years, and even my mom worked there for a while, way back—so I've been told. Dad says they've always treated their employees like disposable goods, and I wish I could say that surprised me. I guess being a town landmark for decades has given the Brannaghs big heads. But that's not who Max is. He's the diamond in the rough.

I pull my car keys from my bag as a bead of sweat trickles down my neck—it's so hot already, unseasonably so for June. I'm starting the engine when my phone buzzes with a text. It's from my sister Vaughan:

I will personally kill you if you are late for tonight.

I roll my eyes and drop my phone in the cup holder. *Obviously* I'm not going to be late. I pump the gas, buzz the windows all the way down. I'll take wind over AC whenever I can—I like things natural. Authentic.

The thing is I love Vaughan, she's a great big sister, but it irks me how even now she has to take that older-and-wiser high ground. There are only three years between us and I'm thirty now, for crying out loud. Maybe Mara's been needling her: *where's your sister, have you spoken to your sister, why isn't your sister here?*

But they should trust me enough to know I wouldn't be late for this. Mara might get on my last nerve sometimes, but I'm not the kind of person who would sabotage her big day. Or Dad's—this is his special day too. Even though things haven't been easy between us lately, I'd never jeopardize tonight.

But it seems like in this family I have an identity I can't shake off, no matter what I do. Middle child. Renegade. *Where did we go wrong with Dinah?* I've thought often enough about what it would be like to be a golden child instead of the black sheep. Pretty great, is my guess. That's why I'm committed to never, ever letting Josie feel less than the apple of my eye.

Thinking of my daughter puts a sudden lump in my throat and I tell myself to get a grip. I don't think of myself as a sentimental person, but it's something about today: the memories, the might-have-beens. And that strange shivery feeling that keeps washing over me, this sixth sense of a storm rolling in. But there's no storm, and the forecast is for a balmy night.

*

Ten minutes later, and there it is rising up ahead of me: my childhood home. It's a handsome old house but rickety, with a roof that leaks and birds' nests in the chimneys. To me, though, it was always a palace. Mom loved it too. Dad says she fell in love with it right from the start, the second she saw the magnolia tree blooming in the front yard. It still blooms, not once but twice a year now: the miracle magnolia, Dad calls it. He says it only started doing that when I was about five years old. It's just a fancy of mine, but I like to think that the miracle is Mom, somehow: a kind of sign that part of her is still watching over us.

What did I say just now about not being sentimental? Today must really be getting to me.

The thing is, three years old isn't old enough to have real memories. Even the ones I have of Mom may just be because of what Vaughan has told me. She was seven when Mom died, and at that age, four years makes a world of difference.

Josie's six now and I can't imagine—God forbid—what her world would be like if she were suddenly to lose me. I couldn't bear to imagine her growing up without me. At least Mom couldn't have foreseen any of what was going to happen. At least she didn't have time to realize all she was losing. The crash happened so fast. I wonder if we were the last thing she thought of before it was all over.

The car clunks over gravel and I ease it into the space beside the magnolia tree and cut the engine.

I don't begrudge Dad the happiness he's found with Mara, but I just can't help thinking today of the might-have-beens. Of the alternate reality where my mom is still alive, and of the party she and Dad might have thrown for *their* anniversary if they'd had the chance. What would it have been this year—their thirty-fifth, maybe?

I wonder if Dad has been thinking of her today.

I wonder if he thinks of her every anniversary.

I bet Mara would hate that thought.

I get out of the car and slam the door. Through the hanging ivy I can see into the back garden, the circular tables already laid out, a couple of neighborhood kids Mara has hired for the day to help. I'd have thought Mara would be out there with them, issuing instructions in her Manager Voice, but I don't see her or Dad out here. I scan the garden for Josie too but there's no sign of her. She's probably up in our room with a book. I used to spend so many hours in this garden as a kid, but my daughter is more of an indoor creature.

I pause at the door, looking up at the house again before I step inside. The brickwork crenellated with ivy; the windows like eyes in a beloved face. I know why Mom fell in love with these four walls.

It comes over me again, this strange, haunting feeling that won't leave me alone today. I'm looking at everything like it's the last time—which is absurd.

This old house isn't going anywhere. But I can't shake this flicker of foreboding.

A shadow moves across a bedroom window upstairs, Lottie's window. My younger sister—my half-sister, technically. Mara's daughter. We used to be best friends...once upon a time.

Life is weird like that, the way it upends things you thought would always be the same.

The things you thought you could count on forever.

My phone pings again—probably Vaughan, still wearing her big-sister boots. I draw in a long breath and square my shoulders. I'm about to open the door when I hear Mara's voice through the open window.

'George, just snap out of it, will you?' She sounds impatient, on the verge of losing her cool in a very un-Mara like way. Dinah's a grown woman, this can't go on.'

I inhale sharply. *Me?* What have I done now?

But whatever Dad mumbles in response, he's too far away for me to hear. I remind myself, with a big effort of will, that nothing good ever came from eavesdropping, and I step back quietly from the window and trudge around to the side door. I check my watch: an hour until the guests start arriving. Time to face the music.

I push open the door and step inside.

Chapter Two
Lottie

I exhale as I watch Dinah disappear through the side door and stand back from the window. I run my hands over the thick drapes, the blue silk fabric Mom picked out for me when I was a teenager. It's weird having the house full again. Dinah and Josie in Dinah's old bedroom and Vaughan down the hall in hers. Vaughan's room got turned into a workout room years ago, so the futon's pushed up against an exercise bike and an array of dumbbells gathering dust. The dumbbells were Daddy's impulse purchase, and the truth is he's just not a workout kind of guy. More of a 'whiskey on the rocks in my recliner' kind of guy, if we're honest.

I smile, remembering him just a couple of hours ago, having his twelve o'clock "breakfast" in a ratty bathrobe as Mom bustled around him, making meaningful comments about the time.

'Relax, Mar,' Dad had yawned, and gave her elbow a squeeze. 'We'll get it done.'

Mom made an impatient noise, which I couldn't blame her for.

I feel the sweat beading at the back of my

neck—it's June, but already August-hot. I turn the AC on, and my phone pings. I smile to myself. That name on my screen still brings the little rush and flutter in my chest.

'Who's texting you?'

I turn around. Mom's standing in the doorway, one hand on the knob.

'Sorry, should I have knocked?'

I sigh, trying not to do it audibly. Mom's just not the knocking type. She cuts her eyes to my phone.

'So? Who're you texting?'

'Just a friend from work,' I say. Mom nods. I don't have any friends from work, but she doesn't know that. I haven't told her about Roman—there hasn't seemed much point, since it's not something that's going to last. But I have to admit I'm enjoying it all the same.

I will the smile off my face in case it stokes Mom's curiosity further. I wish I were harder to read—more like Vaughan, maybe. Vaughan should take up poker or something, she's that good at keeping herself to herself. As for Dinah, she tells you what she's thinking because she *wants* you to hear it, and good luck escaping her frank opinions. But me, I'm the one always trying to hide what I feel and losing.

'You look nice,' I say to Mom, and she does. Mom's a head shorter than I am and small-boned, and even in her sixties has those adorable freckles that Dad says made him fall for her. Her blush-colored dress might look too young on other women her age, but she looks just right. As usual, she looks cool as a cucumber, barely feeling the heat. She never does. Dinah calls her the Ice Queen, but that's not why. Dinah thinks I don't know she has that name for Mom.

'I bought something for you.' Mom smiles. 'Close your eyes, okay?'

I do, and hear a rustle. Tissue paper, or plastic.

'Okay, open them.'

It's a dress. She lifts up the protective plastic so I can see the fabric better, draped over her arm. It's a soft yellow shade, the color of primroses. It's charming, and really not my thing.

'I thought it would be beautiful against your tan,' she says.

I have Daddy's skin that turns a true tan by the end of summer. Mom burns to a crisp if she doesn't lather up with SPF 50 starting in May.

'It's beautiful,' I say. And it is. And yet... I wish she wouldn't do this. I wish she wouldn't plan things for me like this. Does that sound ungrateful? It's just... this is Mom's kind of dress. Not mine. I'd already picked out what I was going to wear: a grey sheath dress, nice and simple. The yellow dress has a sweetheart neckline, a pinched waist, cute little touches here and there that would look great on Mom but fussy on my taller, athletic figure.

'I'm happy you like it.' She smooths the plastic back down over it, gives it a shake so it rustles on the hanger, and looks at it proudly. 'I *knew* it would be perfect on you.'

She's glowing, and I feel guilty for faking my enthusiasm. I lean in and give her a kiss on the cheek—lightly, because I can see she's started to apply her makeup already. She smiles, looking a little surprised. We're not huggy, kissy types in this family.

'I still haven't seen Dinah,' Mom notes, her forehead puckering slightly.

'She just got back,' I say. 'I saw her out the window. She's probably downstairs somewhere.'

'Well, that's a relief,' Mom sighs.

The Dinah Train, we used to say when Dinah was younger. The Dinah Train chooses its own time and its own stops—it arrives when it arrives and not a moment sooner, so good luck trying to schedule it. It used to irritate Mom to no end, but I mostly just felt admiration. I wish I'd ever been so sure of *anything* as Dinah always seemed to be about everything.

Mom heads back downstairs, buzzing with high spirits and to-do lists. I flick on the radio and shake my head to clear my thoughts. I've had this kind of nostalgic feeling all day today—maybe it's seeing Vaughan's and Dinah's rooms in use again. That doesn't happen even at the holidays, everyone stays in their own homes now. I'm the only one still living with Mom and Dad.

For now.

I cast a glance at the envelope sitting on my desk. I'm going to have to tell my parents what's in there sooner or later, and probably sooner. They're going to think I'm crazy. And maybe I am.

I turn back to the yellow dress Mom left hanging over the wardrobe and slip it off its hanger. It rustles and shivers as I slide it over my head, and I turn and examine myself in the mirror. It fits like a glove even if it's really not my style—but this is a day to make Mom happy. And Daddy too, of course, but he'd be happy if I turned up in a paper sack.

I open my wardrobe and scan the bottom of it for the right pair of shoes. I'd love to borrow those little white peep-toes Dinah had on yesterday, but borrowing from Dinah... well, everything with Dinah is tricky these days.

It wasn't always like this, with me and her. There *was* a time when—

Stop, Lottie, I tell myself. There's no point dwelling on that now. I tried once to talk to my sister about it, but if anything, that only drove the chasm wider. So now I just live with, and try to forget how different it used to be.

I go out into the corridor—my room's all the way at the end—and step up to Dinah's door. When I tap there's a childish "come in."

'Josie-bear, is your mom up here?'

Josie looks up from the book on her lap, her little face all lit up and earnest. It's her *I'm-so-deep-in-a-story-I've-forgotten-my-own-name* face. My niece is an absolute sweetheart and there's no one in our family who doesn't adore her. The beautiful black hair she inherited from Dinah—who inherited it from *her* mother—falls back from her forehead as she looks up at me. Usually it's all over her face in a curtain; Josie's a shy kid, nothing like her mom.

'Narnia?' I say when I see the book cover. 'Haven't you finished them all already?' I remember her ripping through *The Lion, the Witch and the Wardrobe* over Christmas when Mara gave her the set. She's just turning seven, but reading at fourth-grade level already.

Josie nods. 'I have. But second time around is the best!'

Just because of the day we're celebrating, the words stick with me. *Second time around is best.* Divorced people probably say that all the time. But what about when you didn't fall out of love with someone but rather, they were taken from you? I wonder for a moment how Bonnie would feel about all this celebrating going on in her house for her husband's anniversary with another woman.

Josie interrupts my thoughts, saying something I don't quite hear. She's such a quiet little thing.

'Come again?'

'Your dress,' she repeats, ducking her head. 'You look like a princess.'

'Why thank you.' I drop a curtsy. 'What about you, Josie, what are you wearing to the party?'

Her embarrassment gives way to a worried look. 'I don't know… what do you think I should wear?'

17

Poor Josie. She's still so young but I can tell she already worries about letting people down; about not doing what's expected of her. I don't think Dinah fully sees it. Sometimes it's hard to recognize it when people are so different from us. I see it clearly though, because Josie reminds me of myself as a kid.

Josie looks a lot like Dinah did when she was little, but the physical resemblance is deceptive. Dinah was a fearless child but Josie's like a butterfly: hesitant, uncertain. If you're not looking she'll land on your shoulder, but if you hone in on her too much she'll get spooked and fly away.

I look over the selection of clothes Dinah's brought for Josie, all hanging in the closet. Everything of Josie's is ironed and hung immaculately. Dinah might leave her own clothes crumpled and creased, but she'll only have the best for Josie.

Josie tentatively tells me which one's her favorite, and I tell her it's perfect, and she beams.

'Okay,' I glance at the time. 'Time to put on some makeup.'

At the word *makeup*, Josie looks at me like I've mentioned glitter unicorns.

'Want to come into my room and watch?' I remember being her age, watching Vaughan put on makeup, not being able to wait until I was a teenager.

In my room, I pull up the seat at my vanity and pat the bed beside me. Josie hops on cautiously, like she's trying not to hurt the duvet. I can feel her saucer eyes on me as I take out the magical potions. I meet her eyes in the mirror and turn around, hold out the lipstick.

'Want to try?'

Her eyes say it all.

'Here.' I make room for her at the mirror. She scrambles up, and together we dab a pale lipstick oh-so-carefully over her mouth.

'Now go like this.'

She smacks her lips to imitate me.

'And now, the gloss.' We put some on and Josie grins from ear to ear. And then her smile falters a bit and I become conscious of someone in the doorway.

'What's this?' Dinah says. The two words fall like lead balloons.

Josie immediately looks guilty, which makes *me* feel guilty, but I force myself to keep my face unapologetic.

'Josie's helping me get ready,' I say.

'Sweetheart—' Dinah turns and puts out her hand for Josie, who scrambles off the chair. Dinah squats down and wipes off the lipstick from Josie's mouth. 'Not today, okay, sweetie?'

'Okay,' Josie says and scoots out of the room—she can sense it's time to evacuate. Dinah turns to me. I can see the flash in her eyes, the spark of temper she's keeping at bay for now.

It never used to be like this. I was like Josie once: when I was Josie's age and Dinah was twelve, I was the little girl she was never angry with. The kid she'd do anything to protect. The one who could do no wrong.

And then?

Then we grew up, and other things happened.

Now Dinah crosses her arms.

'I *will not* have you turning my *six-year-old* into some kind of...' She gestures. 'Some kind of sexualized *pageant princess,* Lottie. This is not *Toddlers and Tiaras.*' I see her taking in my flouncy new dress, then her anger ebbing away and replaced by what I'm pretty sure is scorn. I can hear the words she doesn't speak. *I won't turn her into a spoiled princess like you.*

I glare at her, not finding the words to match her clever tongue. I've never been as good at this as she is. But then, I never trained for it—I never expected the two of us to be rivals.

Dinah turns on her heel and slowly, I turn back to the mirror. Adrenaline flows through my body. I pick up the lipstick where Josie dropped it, but my hands tremble from the adrenalin rush and suddenly the tube falls from my fingers.

Damn it.

I examine myself in the mirror: one yellow sweetheart neckline, now with a streak of pink lipstick grease.

There's no time to handwash it and let it dry. *Sorry, Mom.*

I open the wardrobe door and take out the grey

dress after all. Dad's jazz music drifts up the stairway, setting my veins tingling with its lush, unpredictable riffs. I turn off the AC and for a quick moment, slide up the pane and stick my head out of the window. Guests are starting to arrive. I see Bonnie's magnolia, pride of place in the front yard. Standing sentinel, watching over us all.

Bonnie's presence seems so strong in this house sometimes—maybe too strong, if that isn't a horrible thing to say. There are signs of her everywhere. She's the one who converted the kitchen, knocking down the interior wall and making it the heart of the house where everyone still gathers. She's the one who chose the bird-patterned wallpaper for the hall bathroom that, when we replaced it after years of wear-and-tear, we had to match *exactly* so that Dinah wouldn't have a fit. She's the one who planted the magnolia, and the roses in the back.

Bonnie, what would you think of all this?

But the cloudless sky has no answer.

I lower the sash, turn back to the mirror. The grey sheath dress needs something more. I reach for a different lipstick—not the soft blush shade I gave to Josie. The one I reach for is one I almost never wear. I pluck it from the back of the bunch and sweep it on, blood-red, plum-ripe.

My war paint. *Now* I'm ready for battle.

Let the games begin.

Chapter Three
Dinah

I tip back the last sip in my glass and waylay a waiter for some more sparkling wine, but he looks at me apologetically and holds up an empty bottle.

'Yeah... poor timing is kind of my thing,' I say, and he laughs nervously and promises to get me on the next round.

The guests are arriving in a steady stream now, the garden filling up fast, sparkling wine being poured for everyone who walks in. Dad and Mara are at the heart of it all, greeting everyone and being thoroughly monopolized. Mara's in her element, of course. Children are skittering around the grass, darting behind the tables, almost invisible—just the tops of their hot little heads bouncing over the sightline. I look around for Josie. I tried to get her to go and join them a few minutes ago, but she's not really a mingler.

I'm so proud of how smart my daughter is, and it's a blessing that she can entertain herself so easily, but all the same I wish she didn't *always* have her nose stuck in a book. I just worry that I should be doing something to help her be more... robust. To get used to the rough-and-tumble of the real world and help her build up her courage. I don't want her to ever get to a place in her life where there's a safe road and a right road, and she chooses the wrong one from lack of confidence.

Because I've taken that wrong road once before.

I pause for a moment and close my eyes. It's the scent of magnolia drifting suddenly across the garden. I inhale deeply, drawing that sweet childhood smell into my lungs. If I didn't open my eyes I could be five years old again. That edgy feeling swirling in my stomach all day is finally starting to abate. Maybe I *will* enjoy this party after all. The least I can do is try.

And then I feel a big hand land on my shoulder and there's a gravelly throat-clearing.

'Dad!' I whip around.

He flicks at my hair, which I've left half-down despite the heat.

'That mane,' he says. 'Just like your mother's.'

There's that damned lump back in my throat again. A quick swallow of wine helps it disappear.

Dad's side of the family is where Vaughan and Lottie get their genes—his grey eyes, high forehead and aquiline nose. When he wants to—and sometimes even when he doesn't—the way he looks down that nose can give him a very disapproving air. I feel like I've been on the receiving end of that disapproval too often in the last six months, pretty much since Max and I started dating.

I get why Dad wasn't happy to see me start dating again. The breakup with Jeff smashed me into little pieces. But that was years ago now, surely I'm allowed another shot at being happy? Part of me thinks it's really about Josie: that Dad somehow reckons I can't be a full-time working mom *and* have time for a love life. Which would be pretty hypocritical if you ask me, considering that Dad found time to meet and marry Mara less than five years after Mom died.

But this is Dad's special day, so I guess for right now, we're ignoring the friction that my love life has caused between us.

'Looks like Mara's having a whale of a time,' I say. We both look over at where she's holding court near the back doors, a circle of admirers around her as she gestures with a glass of bubbly in one hand.

'She *is* in her element, isn't she?' Dad says. He either doesn't hear the edge in my voice, or is ignoring it. I didn't actually mean to sound sharp. It's just Mara has this way of ruling the roost wherever she is, that somehow gets to me. Suddenly I remember the words I heard outside the door earlier. *Dinah's a grown woman. This can't go on.* What has Mara got between her teeth now?

Before I can ask Dad about it, he speaks.

'Dinah—I have something I want to talk to you about.'

I raise my eyebrows.

'I'm all ears.'

'You're staying the night, right? Maybe tomorrow, then. Before you and Josie head home.'

'Dad.' I laugh a little. He sounds so formal. 'We only live thirty minutes away. You make it sound like we're not going to see you for months.'

He frowns. 'Well, this is important.'

'Okay,' I say, starting to frown myself.

He nods, then winces.

'Hold this, would you?' He hands me his champagne flute and puts a hand to his temple. There's a tiny tremor in it I hadn't noticed before. Just age? It hurts to see, though.

'Are you okay?'

'Damned headache,' he says.

'You, a headache?' Dad and Mara are famously hardy. We tease them about their off-the-charts pain tolerance. As a teenager I learned to buy my own stash of painkillers to deal with the cramps and migraines that only I, never my sisters, seemed to get.

'It'll pass,' he says.

I look him over. He doesn't look great, if I'm honest. He's sweating pretty hard, although I guess that's inevitable in this heat. I'm grateful I get to wear a floaty summer dress instead of a long-sleeved suit.

'You're sure?' I say.

He nods, and winces again. 'I just need a minute.' He points at his champagne glass. 'Better you finish that than me, though.'

I see something catch his eye across the garden then, and he nods. I follow his glance and see Mara's signaling to him. *Mingle, George, mingle!* I imagine her saying as I watch Dad walk away.

I sigh and look around for Vaughan again. The neighbor she was chatting to has wandered off, so I sweep in and join her before anyone else can start bending her ear. I lean in to clink my glass—well, Dad's glass—with hers.

'So are you already looking forward to this being over?'

'*Di,*' she says in her warning voice, but I see the corners of her mouth tick up.

Vaughan sweeps back her fine, ash-blonde hair. My older sister is exactly what Lottie will look like in ten years. They're cut from the same cloth, Vaughan and Lottie, down to those silver-grey eyes. *My silver girls,* that's what Dad calls them. I remember when we were little he'd play that Simon and Garfunkel song about bridges over troubled water, and when they got to the line *sail on, silver girl,* he'd pick up Lottie and sail her through the air. She was the littlest of course, easy to lift. But I wished sometimes he'd do that with me.

Even back then, despite the age gap, you could see how Lottie was like a do-over of Vaughan, and now twenty years later they both look like they could be professional dancers or basketball players or something: toned and tall and all-American looking. Not me. I'm the short one; the one with the hips; with the near-black hair that the boys used to call 'witch hair' when I was a kid. I don't have

Vaughan's or Lottie's neat little features and perfect noses.

Sometimes I think the difference between my sisters and me is as simple as the body I was born into. You look at Lottie or Vaughan and you think *discipline*, you just do. Their exactly-proportionate limbs, their pin-straight hair. They look like they woke up ironed. I'm the one with the wild hair, the big voice, the little extra in my chest and butt, none of which I asked for; none of which I chose just to be 'sassy'. My body just happened that way. I don't know, maybe once everybody started seeing me a certain way, I grew the personality to fit it.

I quaff the last of my sparkling wine.

'Dad doesn't seem like he's doing too well,' I say to Vaughan. 'He said something about a headache.' We both watch him greet the newest couple to arrive, pumping their hands in his hearty way. It's that golden hour, a light that makes the garden seem rich with secrets.

I think of *my* secret, upstairs hidden in a box.

'He seemed okay to me,' Vaughan says, surprised. She side-eyes me. 'But... did he say anything to you about an announcement?'

I take my eyes off the garden, and someone's toddler who's uprooting fistfuls of grass unsupervised, to look at Vaughan.

'What kind of announcement?'

She shrugs.

'Don't ask me. He was being kind of mysterious

about it.'

Huh. I glance back over at Dad. *Announcements* aren't really his style—that sounds more like Mara's thing. I assume it's related to whatever he wanted to talk to me about later. He's being so mysterious today. Not like him.

'You're empty.' Vaughan nods at my glass and holds up her own. 'Will I get us refills?'

I shake my head.

'I'll go in. I want to go in and check on Josie anyway.'

Vaughan nods.

'Check on the hors d'oeuvres while you're at it, will you? I'm starving over here.'

I roll my eyes. 'Yes, madam.'

Vaughan smirks at me and I can't help but grin back. If I didn't love her so much it'd be sickening, how Vaughan did it all so *right*: valedictorian; field hockey captain; early decision to UPenn; a string of well-behaved, upstanding boyfriends culminating in Mitchell, whom she married right out of law school. I rack my brains, trying to think of even *one* boyfriend before Mitchell that wasn't the clean-shaven, well-mannered, mothers-love-'em type. No, Vaughan's never put a foot wrong.

She's also the peacekeeper in this family. When Mara and I would go head-to-head when I was a teenager, Vaughan knew just how to calm me down and get Mara to back off. Now that I'm older I try really hard not to put her in that situation any more.

The truth is Mara and I have never really got along—I know she didn't *ask* for two young stepdaughters thrown into the mix when she fell in love with Daddy, but she doesn't get to change the reality. None of us do.

My little sister's a different story, though. When she was little Lottie was adorable—there was no way not to fall for those feathery blonde ringlets, those big eyes. I'd just turned six when she was born and was madly in love with her from the start. When she was a kid she used to follow me around everywhere and it didn't even annoy me, which for a teenager is saying a lot.

But then things changed. Things happened. And somehow... somehow it became too late for those things to change back. Unexpectedly, I feel my eyes growing hot, and I shake the old thoughts away.

I wind my way through the guests on the lawn, the women in cotton prints, the men in linen shirts. So many bright colors. I'm reminded for a moment of Bud and Branch, of arriving in the mornings and unloading our beauties from the walk-in fridge at the back—roses, tulips, fat bright daisies—surrounding myself with their color and light.

I squeeze through the kitchen door and find a space to put the empties down, then head up the staircase to the first floor. My room is in the middle, between Vaughan's and Lottie's—middle child, middle room. The door's open.

'Jojo?'

I step inside and feel a chill. Mara's standing at the desk by the window. The lid's raised as she roots around inside.

'Mara, what are you doing?'

Because all I can think about is the box. *My* box. My secret. Tucked in there on impulse, in the desk I used to study at in high school. Away from curious eyes—or so I thought.

Mara eases the lid back down and turns around, eyebrows raised.

'I'm getting my checkbook to pay the caterer.'

But—

'You're in my room,' I say, my voice high and tight. *The box,* I'm thinking. *Did she see it?*

'Dinah,' she exhales, voice crisp. 'It hasn't been "your" room for ten years.'

I stare at her.

'Well, thanks for letting me know where I stand in this family.' It comes out before I can think twice about it.

There's a beat, and Mara looks... remorseful? Impatient? She opens her mouth to say something, then apparently thinks better of it. She just sighs and edges past me to the door.

When she's gone I sag onto the bed. It takes a moment to catch my breath. I probably shouldn't have been so sharp. I just panicked.

I go over to the desk, lift the lid. The box is still there.

I drop the lid back down with a bang. *She won't say anything,* I tell myself.

She better not.

*

There's a dinging sound drifting through from the garden, a fork against glass. Josie and I emerge from the kitchen and wind our way through the crowd back to Vaughan. She takes Josie's hand—my daughter was in the attic, it turns out, watching the party from on high.

'There you are. Time for toasts.'

Mara and Dad are standing in the middle of the lawn, and Lottie's there beside them, fork in hand—she's obviously the one who's been dinging her glass.

Dad passes a hand across his brow. He looks red-faced, uncomfortable. He pulls at his collar. I wonder if his headache is getting worse. The hand holding his glass shakes, and he stumbles a little as he puts it down on the table. Poor Dad. Maybe it's not the heat, or the headache. Maybe it's just the emotion of the moment. He clears his throat.

'I'm so glad,' he says, and stops. He wipes his forehead again. 'I'm so glad you're all here—that *we're* all here, together, today.'

I close my eyes, breathe in the scent of the garden. I find Vaughan's hand with mine and squeeze it. She's looking at me when I open my eyes, surprised. She doesn't know I'm imagining the alternate universe, the one where Mom stayed alive.

'You're right,' Vaughan mutters. 'Dad really doesn't look well.'

'I'm glad in particular,' Dad goes on. 'Because there's something I want to mention tonight. Something I want to share with you all.'

He looks at Mara, and the way she's looking back at him I can tell right away he's gone off-script. Dad isn't usually one for public speaking anyway—I thought he'd let Mara do all the talking. But now he's standing there looking out over us all, and he looks so intent, so focused, even as he rubs his hand across his sweat-beaded forehead. He grabs a water glass from the table and knocks back a gulp.

He swipes at his forehead again. 'I,' he says. 'I....'

His voice sounds tight, effortful, like it's a strain to keep going, and his face is flushed.

It's quiet in the garden now. Even the birds have stopped singing. I wonder what's happening, why my skin is all goosebumps despite the heat, why time seems to be crystallizing to a single, fine point. And then Dad wipes his forehead again and his hand is shaking, shaking so very hard.

And he looks at me, and I see the look in his eyes. *Glassy*, I think, and that's still where my brain is at as his knees buckle and the glass in his hand drops like a grenade, an explosion of deafening silence.

My father is lying face-forward in the grass.

'Somebody call an ambulance,' a voice shrieks.

And the world as I know it ends.

Chapter Four
Lottie

Breathe, Lottie. Breathe.

But I can't breathe, I can't anything. Vaughan's car hurtles through traffic, and there's just the sound of Josie asking questions in the back. I see them in the mirror: Dinah, wild and pale as a ghost, with Josie clutched on her lap. Beside me Vaughan doesn't take her eyes off the road, hunched over the steering wheel like she can press the car forward with the weight of her body. Mom went in the ambulance with Daddy.

The paramedic was so calm. The stretcher looked so small. I hear again the back doors of the ambulance shutting, their smart little snap. How could such an innocent sound be so terrifying? Mom was like a robot, nodding at everything the EMT said like it was a fire drill. Vaughan kept her head, herding the rest of us into her Prius and hitting the gas as the ambulance blasted down the road. We managed to keep it in sight for a block or two and then it flew through a red light and disappeared, and a thread in my chest stretched and broke.

'Is Grandpa going to be all right?' Josie says in the back seat. I lift my eyes to the rearview mirror. No one says anything for a second.

'We don't know yet, darling. We hope so.' Dinah says quietly, and reaches her arm tighter around Josie. Dinah doesn't believe in lies, even the reassuring ones most parents would invoke at a time like this. I wish someone would lie to me right now though, take my hand and say, *it's all going to be okay. It's all going to be just fine.*

I flash back to that neighbor kid standing across from me when it happened. Her hand gripping the tray of hors d'oeuvres, her puppy-fat teenage face suddenly ashen with fear. The way she caught my eye and I knew she was thinking how terrible it would be to be me just then. I feel an uncontrollable wave of envy. She'll be telling this story tonight to her friends, she'll get to walk away from this nightmare and I won't.

'Left, Vee,' Dinah chokes out from the back seat. We're at the hospital entrance and there's a sign that says *Visitor Parking* and another that says *ER.* A sign for everything, and no one to tell us what to do.

We swing into a space, and Vaughan kills the engine.

Inside the building, the man at the desk tell us George Spencer has been brought to Cardio.

We hurry down the corridor and Dinah rams the elevator button with her fist, again and again.

'Cardio,' Vaughan says.

We look at her.

Heart attack. We're all thinking it.

The elevator pins open and we pile in, and as we wait time seems to be speeding up and slowing down, the seconds tripping over themselves. I realize I know nothing about the statistics. How many people die of heart attacks? Can you just have a... a *mild* heart attack?

That wasn't a "mild" heart attack, Lottie. I remember the way he keeled over in the garden, his frozen look of panic and fear, the single moment that seemed to stretch forever.

The elevator spits us out and we rush in a stop-start way, looking for signs, for a nurse's station, for—

'Mom!'

She turns around, and her face is hollow, already changed. We all stop abruptly, and Mom looks at us with this horrible blankness across her face.

'What did they... where is he?' I say. 'Is he going to be—' I can't say *okay*.

Mom doesn't reach for me. She just stands there, her head nodding slightly like one of those bobble-head dolls Dinah used to have.

'They said it's a cardiac arrest,' she says. 'They—' She takes a breath. 'They did a—an angiogram.' She says the words carefully, like a foreign language she's being tested on. Like the problem is the words, not the reality we're suddenly living. 'They said he needs emergency bypass surgery. He's in there right now.'

Dinah lets out a hiccup of fear. I feel it too.

Emergency means life-or-death. Emergency means not a second to spare, top priority for all the worst reasons.

'How long is it supposed to take?' Dinah manages to say. 'The surgery.'

Mom blinks, like the question is hard to process. It's like she's underwater, not quite hearing us. I think of Dad on an operating table. Is it like in the movies? Will it be cold in there, will he be in pain?

'I don't know, Dinah,' Mom says. 'Hours, I think. I think it depends.'

On what they find.

On how bad it is.

I swallow.

'Mommy,' Josie pulls at her hand in Dinah's grip. 'Mommy, you're hurting me.'

Dinah blinks, loosens her grip. 'Sorry, darling.'

'What's a bypass?' Josie's eyes move from one to the other of us.

I catch Vaughan's pained expression. Josie shouldn't be here, but there's nowhere else for her to go. *We should have left her at home with Dad*, some slow-to-catch part of my brain thinks, and then I realize what I've done and feel sickened. I close my eyes, wait for the stomach lurch to pass.

Daddy is what holds this family together. What on earth would we do without him?

*

There's no one else in the waiting room. The room feels cavernously big, freezing cold from the air

36

conditioning, with dog-eared magazines from last Christmas cluttering the table. Our heads snap up every time someone passes in the corridor outside, but they don't stop.

Vaughan's on her phone. I guess she's WebMD-ing *bypass surgery* and *cardiac arrest* and *angiogram*, which is more than I have the stomach to do. I'm too scared of what I'd find.

Then the door rattles and a woman in a white coat steps through. She casts her eyes over our group and I see us for a moment through her eyes: wife, daughters, granddaughter.

Please 'wife.' Please not 'widow.' Don't let Mom be a widow.

'Mrs. Spencer?' the woman settles her gaze on Mom, and through the haze of fear I wonder why she's addressing only Mom, why not all of us.

Maybe it's protocol, you have to address next of kin if someone...

Don't say dead, my brain pleads.

'We've been working on getting your husband's heart going again.'

I feel my own heart contract and stutter.

Going *again?* I see the shock on everyone's face.

'His body has undergone a huge trauma, Mrs. Spencer. His heart is beating again, but I can't say much about longer-term outcomes at this point. He may not regain consciousness for some time.'

'What kind of time,' Dinah says, her voice sharp. The doctor pauses, then turns her way.

'That depends on a lot of factors. He's intubated right now. He's unlikely to be off the ventilator in the next twenty-four hours. We'll take it day by day.'

I'm thinking about the rest of what she said. *Longer-term outcomes. Can't say much.* The way she said, *His heart's beating again,* like she almost wanted to add *for now.* Did anyone else hear it that way, or was it just me? I look around at the dazed faces.

'Can we see him?' Vaughan's voice is tremulous.

'We'll be moving him to the Cardiac Care Unit post-op, you'll be able to visit him'—the doctor checks her watch—'in the morning.'

I can feel the edge of despair in the room then, as though if we don't see Daddy with our own eyes now he might disappear, as though we can't afford to let the night go by.

'Someone will speak to you about CCU visiting regulations.' She looks at us all. 'But for now you might want to go home, rest, and come back first thing in the morning.'

'Absolutely not,' Dinah says. The doctor just blinks at her. Whatever natural sympathy might be there is locked behind a wall of detached professionalism. I want to take her by the shoulders and shake her and tell her, *This is my father. How would you feel?*

'When will—when will we know more?' I say. 'About his condition.'

'We'll know more with time, as his body tells us more.' She looks from me to Mom. 'Mr. Spencer is not a young man. You need to be aware... what he's just experienced, it's been'—she pauses—'very hard on his body. A cardiac arrest is a very severe event.'

I feel like being sick again. Mom's staring at the wall, like she's alone in the room. Instead I find Dinah's eyes locking on mine, her freckles livid, her dark hair wild as a banshee's. When our eyes meet there's a shock of intimacy, of directness, that we haven't had in years. Because we're both thinking the same terrible thought.

He might die.

He really might die.

When the doctor's gone it's like a spell is broken and we all look around at each other. Josie's eyes are wide as saucers. I feel like I could be her age: it's like I can feel the last two decades slipping away from me, until I'm small and helpless once more. Dinah's gripping her hand again, hard enough that Josie's fingers are white, but this time she doesn't seem to notice.

It's so very cold in here.

*

Vaughan doesn't speak on the drive home. She's alone in front; I sit in the back with Josie's head in my lap. It's pitch dark outside. I don't even know how many hours we were in the hospital. We left Mom and Dinah there, side by side in the stiff waiting-room chairs, in their crumpled party clothes and worn-out makeup.

How can this all be happening?

To *Dad*?

We can't lose him, I think up at the dark sky, as if the world outside the car window can be persuaded.

At home Vaughan and I help Josie change and tuck her in. We wait until she falls asleep again, and to my surprise it only takes a moment. She must have been exhausted. When she drifts off we look at each other. Now it's just us, alone with the truth. We go back downstairs and Vaughan uncorks a bottle of bourbon.

'Want one?'

I nod. I don't know how it's possible to feel so exhausted yet so wide awake. I take the glass from her and see the shake in her outstretched hand. We sit at the kitchen table like actors waiting for our cues.

The truth is, Dad's the thing that holds this half-and-half family together. He's the center of it all. Without him here, I don't know how Mara and Dinah would manage together—and Vaughan too, in her quiet way. Would my sisters just drift away? Would we fall apart, without him?

'It's worse than a heart attack, you know,' Vaughan says.

I snap my eyes back to her.

'A cardiac arrest,' she goes on. 'It's not the same thing. It's… the recovery rates are lower.'

I'm wishing she hadn't said that.

'What are they?' I say despite myself.

Her eyes drop from mine and she shrugs, not very convincingly.

'It's Google,' she says. 'We should wait to hear from the doctors.'

I swallow.

'Lottie...' Vaughan finally says. 'What do you think he was going to say?'

I look up.

'Dad,' she says. 'The speech. The big announcement. Remember?'

And I do remember—the bright look in his eye, the electricity in the air, and the edge in his voice like he was going to spill a secret.

Secrets don't leave the body easily. I think of the secrets I've carried; of the one I still carry. I picture how deeply it's become embedded in me. I imagine it leaving me now, ripping me open. An exit wound like a bullet hole.

But that's a silly thought. A fantasy. Secrets don't kill us. Lies don't kill us.

Don't they, Lottie? a little voice says. *Are you so sure?*

I look back at Vaughan.

'He'll tell us,' I say firmly. 'When he wakes up.'

George

George isn't used to the dark.

He's in a strange place, wherever he is. Why is it so dark? And why can't he remember how he got here? He tells himself to move forward, but he can't tell if his feet are obeying. He takes a step, or thinks he does.

Slowly does it, George.

It's so dark, and so quiet. There's no one else around.

Or… is there? He thought he saw her just now. An outline, a wisp in the darkness. Someone he used to know. Someone he used to love. Someone who'd been waiting a long time, to welcome him or to punish him.

'Are you there?' he says into the darkness, but it doesn't answer.

'Are you there?' he repeats. 'Can you hear me?' And his voice echoes back to him in the dark. Hear me. Hear me.

Hear me.

And George takes another step into the blackness.

Chapter Five
Dinah

'Di?'

I groan.

Vaughan stands over me, the overhead electric light behind her, her hair dangling in unwashed blonde hanks.

'Di, he's in the ICU. They said we can go see him. Do you hear me, Dinah?'

I bolt upright. My neck screams in protest from the way I slept curled in this awful chair.

'What time is it? How is he? What did they say?'

Vaughan blinks at me. I've never seen her look this haggard. The shadows under her eyes are dark and the yellow light in here makes her look sickly.

'It doesn't—it doesn't sound too good. Mara's in there now. They'll let us in when she comes out. They've put in some kind of pump, the doctor said. Something to help his heart squeeze better. I guess they have to wait and see if it'—she pauses—'If it works.'

I wipe the crust of drool from the side of my mouth, push my unbrushed hair from my face. I look towards the door, like Dad might walk in any minute, humming Charles Mingus and jiggling the change in his pocket.

'Okay. Let's go,' I say, trying not to let my voice betray me. I don't want to let Vaughan down. I don't want it to remind either of us how terrified I am of what we'll find.

*

The ICU is loud, but the moment I see Dad it's like everything goes quiet. It's hard to see *him,* past all the stuff that now surrounds him like a grey forest. The monitors, the cables, the huge oxygen mask over his face. His hair flops in a wave over his forehead, brushing his closed eyelids. Vaughan gently moves the hair back from his face, and I swallow. I'm supposed to be the gutsy one, the fierce one, but right now I don't know if I can bring myself to reach out and touch him, though Vaughan does it so easily. He doesn't look right; he doesn't look peaceful. The way he's lying is too symmetrical, his arms tugged down by his sides like a doll's, as if they were placed that way by someone else. I guess they were. I picture the nurses maneuvering my unconscious father into this bed; the indignities already inflicted on that poor body.

'Dad, it's us,' Vaughan says quietly. 'Me and Dinah. We're here. We're really happy to see you.'

I'm in awe of how she's holding it together.

'You had a really long surgery but you're out the other side now, Dad,' she goes on. 'Now you just have to get better. You have to get better and come back to us.'

Her voice doesn't even shake.

44

'Vaughan,' I whisper. A whisper's all I can manage over my constricted throat; it's all I can do without my voice breaking and my heart breaking right along with it.

'I'm sorry,' I say, because I know now I can't be in this room. I *can't*. I'll lose whatever strength I'm pretending I still have. And I have a daughter to be strong for.

'I'm so sorry, Vee. I just—I can't do this.'

She looks at me.

'I'll wait outside,' I say. 'I'm sorry.'

But it's not her I'm speaking to.

I'm sorry, Dad. I'm so sorry.

*

In the car we don't talk about how I left; how I didn't even say goodbye to Dad or tell him I'd be back soon. How I wasted the precious fifteen minutes we'd been given.

My phone pings and I fish it out of the silk purse I'm still carrying from last night, sitting in my lap along with the high heels I wrenched from my feet. As for the dress, I will never, ever wear it again. It used to be one of my favorites but now it belongs to the worst night of my life.

Vaughan cruises to a stop in our driveway and I look out at Mom's magnolia.

Mom, please do something, I think. *If you're listening. If you're there. Please do something.*

My phone pings again, reminding me of the unread message. It's from Max.

Are you okay, Di? What's the latest?

I told him about Dad's collapse last night—just the bare bones, I didn't have the strength to call him and relive it all out loud.

I stare at the message. I'm not okay, not even close, and I don't know what the news is.

He's in the ICU now, I text back.

My phone buzzes in response.

Can I see you? I'll drive over.

Vaughan pulls the emergency brake and snaps the car door open. Yesterday's surge of heat has died, and now it's early morning, cool. The gravel is sharp under my bare feet. The pain is comforting.

'Mommy!'

Josie's in the doorway. Mussed hair, sleepy eyes, and a new uncertainty written across her little face. This must be scaring her so much.

'Jojo.' I open my arms, and she skitters across the gravel and buries herself in them. I see the shadow of Lottie behind her in the kitchen doorway.

'Is Grandpa better yet?' Josie's muffled voice comes through my shirt.

I kiss the top of her head. 'Not yet, darling.'

'But soon?' the little voice says.

'We hope so, darling,' I say, because I don't believe in promises I can't keep. 'We really, really hope so.'

Lottie steps out onto the porch, car keys in hand. She's dressed for the hospital and despite her height looks waiflike in her loose sweater and jeans, wet hair in a braid. I see a flash of the person who used to be my baby sister. Back when we were a different kind of family. Back when everything was different.

'How was it?' she says. 'How was he?' She swallows. 'Mom said… she said they're using some kind of pump on his heart.'

'He'll get through it,' I interject, and she and Vaughan both look at me. 'He will,' I repeat. 'He'll get through this.'

They look at me and at each other. Lottie nods but I can tell it's only to pacify me. We all know that I *don't* know. None of us knows anything. We can only hope.

Lottie lets herself out and the door closes softly behind her. I hear the distant snick of the car door and the crunch of wheels down the driveway.

'Jojo, have you had breakfast?'

Josie shrugs, which means *yes, but*. My little girl is skinny as a string bean but is somehow a bottomless pit for food.

The kitchen's always been our family room, the room where we discuss things, celebrate things. Our kitchen table has seen every family conference, every heartbreak… it's seen Vaughan and me through our Spaghetti-O years, and Lottie through her college exams. *The heart of the house,* Dad likes to say. It was Mom's idea to knock two rooms into one, replacing the original, tiny kitchen with a big bright room that runs the length of the house. Its yellow walls catch the sun, but even they don't look cheery today. Today, even the heart of the house looks like its dying.

Vaughan fills the toaster and I scoop out the coffee. Josie clambers onto the counter stool at the kitchen island. I stroke her skinny arms, smooth her hair back with the palm of my hand. When the toaster pops, Vaughan puts the four slices on a plate and pushes them our way. I push two back.

'I'll eat later.'

I spread the remaining two with raspberry jelly and watch Josie crunch down on them in her voracious way. For a kid so shy about almost everything, my little girl is shameless about her hunger—and somehow the sight of it is so reassuring, so *normal*, that without warning I tear up.

Then I go to pour the coffee and when I look at my mug it's the one that says *Coltrane is King*, one that I gave to Daddy when I was a teenager. I glance out the back window to the garden.

That stupid, stupid party.

Come on, Dinah. The party didn't cause this.

But what if the party was the trigger? All the chores. All the planning. All the stress.

'Dinah?'

I look up.

Vaughan's stirring sugar into her coffee, which she doesn't usually do. It's a sign she's running even lower than empty.

'I think we should stay here for now. At the house.'

'Stay?' I echo. Vaughan and Mitchell live in Connecticut, a three-hour drive away.

'I just think... we're closer to the hospital, you know?' She looks at me. 'And this way we can all stay together. For now at least,' she adds.

I'd sacrifice any amount of days, weeks, months for Dad to get better. But how long can we put everything on hold for? How long can we live in limbo?

'We can play it by ear,' Vaughan goes on. She's speaking low, still Josie must have heard.

'Are we staying here, Mommy?' she pipes up.

I think of her school, of her routine. But I can call the school, see if they can get her on a bus route here. If not, I can drive her. Babette's a compassionate boss. We might be able to rearrange some shifts at Bud and Branch if necessary, and Vaughan and the others will help.

Josie watches me. I can feel her confusion, not sure if this is a fun thing, like a holiday, or a bad thing.

'We could,' I say. 'How would you feel about that, baby?'

Josie nods slowly. There's jelly all around her mouth.

'Baby girl.' I hand her a paper towel, and she dutifully mops her face. I feel the urge to cry again.

I look at Vaughan.

'What about Mitchell?' I say quietly. 'Would he be okay coming here too?'

A shift comes over Vaughan's face then. I don't

know what it means. It's not something I'm used to seeing when she talks about her husband.

'Mitch is traveling,' she says. 'Remember?'

I actually don't remember. I know he declined to come to the anniversary party, and the fact that neither of my sisters were bringing "plus ones" is was what helped me justify it to Max as a "just family" thing. Maybe Vaughan did already tell us about some business trip though, and I forgot. Mitch travels for business a lot. He's an executive at some shipping company and together he and my architect sister are a power couple: tall, well-dressed, good house, nice car—you know the type. I look back at Josie.

'Okay,' I say. 'Let's stay.'

My daughter smiles and pushes her empty plate back towards me. I lift it and stack it in the dishwasher.

The house phone rings then, startling us all. I comfort myself that it's not Mara or Lottie trying to reach us—they'd call our cellphones.

'Probably a robo-call,' Vaughan says, and the tautness in her voice tells me her nerves are just as jangled as mine.

I cross to the old wall-phone Dad and Mara have had since the nineties.

'Hello?' I pick up.

'Hello.' A man's voice, businesslike. 'I'm calling for George Spencer?'

It's like a bad joke.

'I'm sorry,' I say. 'He's not here.'

I'm half-expecting this guy to say something like, *can I speak to whoever makes decisions about your energy supply* or something like that, but he just says to tell George that Matty Atkins called back.

Maybe I should tell him about Dad, but I don't know how to begin to have that conversation. And I don't think I can bear to. Not with a stranger.

'I will. Thanks for calling, Mr. Atkins.'

I put down the phone and turn back to Vaughan's enquiring look.

'Some guy called Matty Atkins,' I manage. 'For Dad.'

The room becomes even quieter, if that's possible. Vaughan looks down at her coffee, gives it a swirl.

'I think that's Dad's lawyer.'

'Dad has a lawyer?' I say.

Vaughan shrugs. 'Dad put me in touch with him a couple years ago, he and his wife wanted a backyard extension.'

I wonder why a lawyer was calling for Dad. *Calling back,* he said. So why did Dad want to speak to a lawyer in the first place?

*

I sink into the ratty old couch in our living room, and lean into Max as he puts his arms around me. It's lunchtime; Mara and Lottie are back from the hospital.

'Are you sure you want to stay here?' Max says. 'You could stay with me if you wanted to.'

He's not as near the hospital as Mara is, but he's still nearer than our place in Rhodesbury. He could take care of Josie while I'm at the hospital. And I know he'd take care of me. It's tempting, but...

'I think Josie should be with her family right now,' I say. 'I think it's better this way.'

Max looks a little pained but doesn't fight it.

'I just want to take care of you, Dinah,' he says. 'I wish I could take you away from all this.'

'I know,' I say, and give him a tired smile. It's something I'm learning to get used to, Max's protective instinct. The way he wants to treat me. I'm not used to thinking of myself as soft and fragile and I don't particularly want to start. But right now I have to admit it feels comforting to be taken care of.

Max Brannagh. The mid-morning light falls over him as he sits on the sofa, his green eyes earnest under his sandy hair. He's still a mystery to me in some ways, his mixture of confidence and anxiety—the things he wants and the things he fears.

I know the family restaurant owned his life for most of his teenage and young adult years. I'm certain that's where his anxious side comes from—always having to worry about adult things like turnover and budget and profit since he was young. He started working there full time just before the bottom fell out of the economy in '08, but they kept going, just about. And then finally a couple of years ago when things were starting to get better at last, his dad sold the whole thing to some outsider.

That hit Max hard. Less than a year later he opened up his own café. I think maybe he doesn't know what to do without something to nurture and try to save.

Like his new business.

Or me.

I swallow and push down that lump in my throat, and Max tightens his arms around me.

'I just never thought this would happen,' I say. 'Not to Dad.'

What I don't say out loud—because I'm bitterly aware now of how foolish it is—is that I thought I'd already had my share of tragedy. Losing Mom so young... I just thought somehow Dad would be around forever. That the universe would balance the scales.

How naive of you, Dinah.

'I just wish there was more I could do,' Max says.

And then he looks at me with those earnest eyes and I see the question he's stopping himself from asking. He must see the look in my eyes, the one that says *I can't handle this right now,* because he closes his mouth again and two hard little dimples appear at the corners as he swallows it down. He stands up.

'Call me,' he says. 'If you need anything.'

*

The others are in the kitchen, zoned out and silent. There's a whole platter of mini-sandwiches in the middle of the table, prepared for the party yesterday but never eaten. I watch Vaughan peel off a piece of crust and roll it between her fingers . The cellophaned tray of little sandwiches just makes me think of a wake.

I sink into a chair beside them and Josie comes over to sit in my lap. I adjust to take her weight and wince. My neck's still killing me from a night slumped in those waiting-room chairs.

'All right, Di?' Vaughan notices.

'My neck,' I say.

'There are painkillers upstairs if you want,' Mara says flatly, not lifting her head from her mug of coffee.

I look at her. Painkillers? In this house?

'Whose painkillers?' I say. Mara and Dad are known for their Spartan ways. They sleep on a mattress that's rock-hard. They like cold showers. Their bath towels are like sandpaper. And they don't do painkillers.

Mara looks up like she's a million miles away.

'Your dad's. They're in our bathroom cabinet.'

Now even Lottie gets it. She stares at Mara too.

'Why did Dad buy painkillers?' I say. She's quiet. 'Mara?'

'He'd been having pain in his chest,' she says.

Her words punch me in the stomach.

'He didn't see a doctor?' Vaughan asks.

'You didn't *tell* us?' I say at the same time.

Mara looks from one of us to the other, then at Lottie. She doesn't even look ashamed.

'We didn't think it was serious.'

'You had him moving tables around!' I explode. 'You had him dragging things up and down stairs and around the garden like a cart-horse, all for that stupid party!'

Mara shakes her head. She answers like a sleepwalker, like the answers don't bother her.

'We didn't think it was anything serious,' she says again. 'He just said he was having some pain around his chest.'

'Baby.' I usher Josie down from my lap. 'Go and watch TV for a minute, okay?'

'You let this happen,' I say, once Josie's out of the room. I see Lottie's face tighten but I don't care. Mara doesn't even react.

'You pushed him into this stupid party,' I say. 'Instead of making him go to a doctor.' I get to my feet and my voice cracks. 'Instead of taking *care* of him.'

'Dinah, come on,' Vaughan says, but I can tell she's holding back some anguish of her own. She agrees with me.

'I have to go,' I say. I need to get out of here before my heart punches right out of my chest and I say or do something I regret. I push back my chair, pluck my keys from the table, and march out the door.

Chapter Six
Lottie

We sit in the silence of the slammed door. Mom doesn't look at me, or at Vaughan. I don't know what to think. Did it really not occur to Dad that it might be something worth looking at—or did he sense something was wrong, and chose denial?

I roll my napkin up and place it on the table.

'I'm going to see how Josie's doing.'

Josie gleefully makes way for me on the couch when I go in. Dinah doesn't let her watch a whole lot of TV, so she's clutching the remote now with a victorious look, both hands wrapped around it in her lap. She pulls a throw over the two of us and we sink into the comforting mind-numb of *Doc McStuffins*. I try to tell myself again that this *is* really happening; that even though it feels like a bad dream I'm going to wake up from any minute, it's not.

Fifteen minutes. Fifteen measly minutes: that's the maximum time, apparently, that's allowed for visiting in the ICU. Too many monitors going off. Too 'disruptive.' Meanwhile the doctors have a look when they speak to us, like they're trying to iron out their faces in case they accidentally give us too much hope.

I don't feel ready for any of this. I don't feel brave, or fierce, or strong. As a kid, Dinah was my protector. And as a teenager, Dad was the one who'd anchor me, build up my courage. Mom was the one who enrolled me in every sport, mounted my trophies, sewed torn uniforms. But Dad was the one who understood when a harsh word from a teammate reduced me to tears, the one who talked me down from my anxiety over an upcoming tournament or guilt over a missed goal.

I need him to show me how to be in the world.

The thing is, this spring I'd been dreaming of escape. I've always been the baby of the family and I've never really left the nest: I went to college nearby, got a job right out of college, stayed at home and started saving. Dad and Mara approved. I think they liked having one kid still at home. But lately I'd been feeling... well, the truth is I hate my job doing customer service support at a software company out in Harrisford. It's lonely and monotonous and sometimes I almost forget I'm a real person, not just a disembodied voice on a phone reading a script to a customer. I kept remembering just before last Christmas when Mom and I drove down to New York, and two hours down the I-87 I saw those signs for the Culinary Institute. I felt this little bubble in my chest just imagining it. I've kept imagining since then. I know how hard chefs and bakers work, it's a punishing rhythm of early starts and late nights. A lot of people would think I'm crazy to want that over what I have now. But the kitchen has always been where I'm happiest, even in the most mundane and repetitive tasks. And the idea of getting up early in the morning to make a perfect loaf of bread? There's just something pure about that.

I hadn't thought of it as anything more than a fantasy, though, until a couple of months ago. Funnily enough it was Roman who urged me to apply. Somehow I ended up blurting out my fantasy future just a week or two into knowing him. He made it sound obvious. *At least apply.* He'd smiled. *You don't need to tell anyone until you get in.* And then I *did* get in. And now the acceptance letter is just sitting on my desk upstairs, stuffed back into its envelope like it never existed.

Which it doesn't, anymore, because I can't go anywhere now. The thought drags me back to the present: whatever happens next, nothing is going to be the same, and I can't leave Mom on her own. I let out a shuddering breath that makes Josie look up from *Doc*. I force a smile for her and she smiles back and wriggles deeper into the blanket.

My sisters grew up fast, losing their mom when they were so little. But me, sometimes it feels like I never had to grow up at all. More and more lately I've been wondering who I'd be if I wasn't the stay-at-home daughter, the one who's never left the nest. I wanted so badly to not just be "George and Mara's youngest daughter" anymore. Now what if I get my wish? What if there *is* no George Spencer anymore; whose will I be then?

I don't even know when was the last time I really asked Daddy about his world—about the garage, his clients, their problems. When I was little I used to love the stories he'd tell at the dinner table, making all the personalities come alive. I used to think of him as a car veterinarian—I pictured the cars like sick puppies, their worried owners bringing them in to get a cough or a temperature seen to. Now it seems like a long time since I listened to those stories. And everything I thought I wanted to shake off, I want back. I want it all back so much.

My phone buzzes in my lap, loud enough for Josie to stir.

Everything ok babe? You been AWOL all day. Still down for Mia's party?

I haven't told Roman about Dad. I wanted to last night, but I couldn't bring myself to pick up the phone and say the words out loud. Tonight I guess some friend of his is having a party. It's hard to believe *that* world is still happening, that not everything has hit pause just because of what's happened to our family.

'Josie, I'm going upstairs for a bit.'

She barely nods, her eyes glazed and sated from TV.

My room is quiet and dark. It's raining outside now. Roman picks up right away when I call. He's on video, and I feel a pang at that easy smile, the way those white teeth sing in his bronze face. In the last twenty-four hours we've become suddenly mismatched—him, light and easy, and me, weighed down by this huge darkness.

'I'm sorry I haven't called,' I say. And then I start to explain. I don't even pick the words, they just tumble out. And then after what feels like a long time I realize Roman hasn't said a word, hasn't interrupted me once. I guess I would have thought he'd jump in with 'helpful' things to say, ideas or proposals, the way other men would have, but instead he's just let me talk myself out till I'm dry. It's the first time I've felt anything like relief all day.

'I'm sorry,' he says then. 'I'm so, so sorry, Lottie.'

Roman and I have only been dating since the end of February, and it's not like it's serious. He's younger than me—twenty-one, just finished college a month ago, for Pete's sake—and going off on a gap year soon. Sometimes I feel like a fool, hanging out with this younger guy who's still basically a student, but it's not like we're planning a future.

Outside the rain starts to pour down hard, and I think of Dinah out there. The weather station has been talking about this storm all week—Mom was so exultant when the forecast said it wouldn't be the day of the party. That seemed so important, just two days ago.

'I'm gonna go,' I say to Roman. 'I'll call you tomorrow.'

I hang up and watch the rain, letting the phone drop to my side.

I know Dinah was crying in the living room with Max earlier. I could see it in her face when she came back into the kitchen. Dinah's fierce—I really only remember seeing her cry once before, which was the summer we built the treehouse and I fell out of it. I was six I guess, she'd just turned eleven. I must have passed out for a minute, and I remember opening my eyes and seeing the blazing blue sky, and Dinah beside me, tears streaming down her face. *I thought you were dead,* she sobbed.

We were so close, back then. We loved each other so much.

I shut my eyes and my thoughts swim back to the hospital, to this morning. Ironic, how after a sleepless night of waiting to see him, I was scared to go in. He looked too still, too quiet, the veins on his hands raised like a carving when I went to touch him. Standing there beside him, all I could think of was that picture book I had as a kid, *The Emperor and the Nightingale.* It was a dark story, a sad story. There was an emperor who was so rich he had everything, and his dearest friend was a nightingale that sang outside his window every morning. But when the nightingale wouldn't sing on demand for him the emperor had a new one built, a mechanical nightingale that would sing without stopping. Then the emperor got deathly ill and he needed the nightingale's song to cure him, but the real nightingale was nowhere to be found. The courtiers brought him the mechanical creature and sat it on top of his chest to sing. But instead of healing him it just weighed him down—deeper and deeper, heavier and heavier, sitting on his chest like a dead weight, like the hunk of metal it really was.

And somehow that was what I thought of, looking at Daddy in that narrow hospital bed. Like there was something sitting on his chest, weighing on him. Keeping him there, unable to come back to us.

I think of him yesterday, the hesitant way he cleared his throat and looked out over the crowd, looking for each of his daughters in turn before he opened his mouth to speak.

What *was* it he was going to say?

I lie back on the bed and stare at the ceiling.

Outside, lightning cracks the sky, and there's still no sign of Dinah.

Chapter Seven
Dinah

I'm drenched to the skin. I walk along the road, watching the dust get washed from the sidewalk and eddy in the gutters. The leaves in the gardens are glossy with rain. My hair's slicked to my scalp, water running down my arms, down my face. I don't care. There's this TV show that Josie and I like to watch, home makeovers where people rip a house apart, finding out what the original structure is underneath all the decades of wallpaper, layers of tiles and linoleum, and plasterboard walls.

You have the knowns, the presenter likes to say. *And you have the known unknowns. And then you have the unknown unknowns.*

That's how I feel now. I'm living in the house of unknown unknowns.

A car slides by me, fast enough to raise a splash of water all along the curb. It's not yet night, but with the dimness of the storm, the cars all have their lights on.

Twenty feet ahead of me, lights blazing, is the McCrae house. It's still in the family, even though Jeff and Oliver's mom moved to Florida a few years back. Oliver and his wife Gillian live there now. Oliver's the homebody, the one who never wanted to leave Birch Bend.

As I get closer, my eye lands on the tall cardboard sign staked into the lawn. Even from here, through the rain, I can make out the big red letters saying *Sale Agreed*. I didn't even know it was on the market.

I can still pick out the room—second left above the door—that used to be Jeff's, and if I closed my eyes I'm sure I could still visualize it right down to the details, those Ramones and Sex Pistols posters he was so fond of; the patched jean jacket hanging on the back of his door.

Jeff McCrae and I met when we tried out for the same band the autumn of junior year. I remember it still—leaves crisp on the ground, all the girls in leather boots. I could sing, sure—but Jeff had a talent that even then you could tell was rare. It felt like art just *watching* him play. I fell head over heels for him, and everything he said made me think he felt the same. We talked about the future all the time, and the life we'd build—how everything would be better, more magical, than what everybody else had. Five years after we met, Josie wasn't exactly planned, but she wasn't *not* planned.

But I don't know. Maybe some small part of me knew even then it wouldn't last. We made it through college—my college, that is; Jeff didn't go because it would have taken too much time away from music—and then when I was twenty-two we moved downstate to New York City. It was where we'd both always wanted to be, but in the end the two years I spent there were probably the most miserable of my life. We could afford so little, and there were no fun nights out in cool bars, or cute little street parks to bring Josie to play in. It was all tired, overworked strangers and dismal fast-food joints, everyone just barely keeping it together with no room left in them to make a friend. And still Jeff spent more and more time on the road, and that road got longer and further every day. And of course it wasn't *just* about the distance. It was about the people I knew he'd meet out there. The women. Jeff's always been strong on charm, less so on self-control.

Things got worse as his music got better. When he played me a new song it made me cry, the sheer fact that he could create something like that. That he could bring such beauty into the world—and how it felt like there was so little of it left for us. I forgave it when he was touring for our anniversary, and the "unmissable" gig that Christmas. But when Josie's third birthday rolled around I helped her blow out the candles alone and realized how miserable I was. I told Jeff I couldn't do this any more—that this was over, and I was going back upstate to Birch Bend.

Jeff still lives down in the city, in Brooklyn last I heard.

Cars swish past me on the road and I think of the car Dad bought for me before I went off to college. It was second-hand, plenty of miles on it, but he'd refurbished it completely, long nights in the garage the week before my high school graduation. When he'd handed over the keys they were on a key-ring that read: *This Princess Saves Herself.* He'd winked at me. *You're my kind of princess, Dinah.*

I pace the road, feeling the small splash of each step as water coats the sidewalk in a film.

Another car coasts by me in the rain, then slows down.

I swipe the rain from my face, and slow my pace as the car comes to a stop near the top of the road. The headlights snap off and I hear the rain-muffled thud of a car door slamming. And it's strange, but the shape of the car, the reddish tinge under the streetlamps… it all looks so familiar.

I squint.

A figure gets out of the car, walks around the side, snaps the trunk open and hauls out a suitcase. The garden sensor light comes on, flooding yellow-white light behind him. And I see what I already knew.

Jeff McCrae may live in New York City but tonight, he's back in Birch Bend.

Rain pelts down around me. I watch the figure in the car-port that's making no move to lug that huge suitcase indoors. Does he see me through this fog of rain?

The figure vanishes.

My phone buzzes in my pocket. Rain drips from every part of me, from my hair and nose and the tips of my fingers. But I pull out my phone, clear the screen of droplets   and see the message from Max.

Thinking of you, it says.

*

Back home, the house is quiet. I shake my dripping shoes from my feet, and use the towel in the guest bathroom to pat down my rain-slick arms and legs. I push back the door of our room and see Josie stomach-down on her bed, book flung to the side—she's fallen asleep reading again.

I pull the sheet up around her, and ease the butterfly clips from her hair and smooth it back. My Josie. I insisted to Jeff if we had a daughter I wanted to call her Josephine, Jo for short, after the second March sister, my childhood heroine. Jeff had laughed and humored me. Now her seventh birthday is just days away—and what a birthday. I never in a million years expected we'd spend it like this.

I drop the hairclips on the nightstand.

Jeff McCrae: I can pinpoint the night when it was clear we were heading for disaster. And I should have ended it then, but it was just when I had begun to suspect I was pregnant. I didn't have the courage, so I swept everything under the carpet and convinced myself the writing wasn't on the wall.

I tiptoe past Josie's bed to the window, open the desk and take out the small black box I tucked inside it, away from prying eyes. I was so mad at Mara yesterday—*snooping,* that was what I thought when I saw her in here, rifling through my desk. Her hand could only have been inches away. I lift the little box into my palm. Ease the lid until it snaps back. And there it is: the white-gold band, a single diamond in the center. It was his grandmother's, he told me. I brush my finger over it. Even in the dim light, it's beautiful.

When I told Max I wasn't ready to say yes his face tightened and I thought we were in for a storm. Then he shook his head and pushed it my way. *Keep it,* he'd said, *tell me when you're ready to wear it.*

It was just five days ago that he asked me that wholly unexpected question. We'd been talking about moving in together for a while, and we were sipping rosé in the backyard, looking at my tomato plants. I was wondering aloud if we'd have a garden in our new place, if they'd survive the transplant—and Max took my hand and held it. *I want to go the whole hog, Dinah,* he'd said. *I want to go all in.*

He had the ring ready and everything.

I can absolutely admit that it was romantic. It *was.* It just wasn't what I had planned for. I just assumed we'd move in together, see how it went, take things slowly. Other people talk about getting *swept away,* but I want my feet on the ground where they can anchor me, where they can support me and keep me strong. I don't want to be swept along on the tide of someone else's will. *I just need to think about it,* I'd said to Max that day. *I would never, ever play games with you,* I told him, trying to take his hand, trying to get his aggravated eyes to stay steady. *I just need some time to think.*

And you know what? Two days ago I was wishing he hadn't asked. I felt that without meaning to he'd forced my hand—*jump now, or lose me*—but in between then and now my world's become a different place. And maybe I'm different. Because all of a sudden Max's words about wanting to take care of me don't sound so old-fashioned. They don't feel like a threat to my independence.

They just feel like a relief.

I look over at my sleeping daughter. At almost seven she's already growing away from me, growing into her inner world of books and stories, the magic that goes on inside her head. I'm so proud that she has all that—I want her to have that deep core, to sustain her through life's challenges when I can't battle them for her—but she needs me less each day. Give it five years.

I don't want to be alone, I think, looking out the window at the dark night. I remember the McCrae house, all lit up and warm. I picture Lottie and Mara sharing cups of chamomile tea in Mara's room. Vaughan and Mitchell, in their perfect home together. I imagine the very worst that could happen, if Dad doesn't come home from the hospital.

No, I don't want to be alone.

I look down at the box and think, *maybe the princess doesn't* always *have to save herself.*

I take a deep breath, pick up my phone, and go

downstairs. I stand in the dark kitchen, scroll to Max's last message, and hit *Call*.

'Dinah?' He picks up. 'It's late. Are you okay?'

'My answer is yes,' I say. 'A big yes.' My eyes smart. 'I want to marry you, Max.'

*

I tell Josie in the car on the way to school the next morning, while we're stopped at a red light. She stops fidgeting with her backpack and looks at me, her little fidgeting body for once perfectly still. Her eyes getting bigger and bigger.

'You and Max are going to get married?'

I pause for a split second. I want to say something like *if that's okay with you*. But that's not fair either. I can't put that weight on her. She looks to me to make the decisions around here.

'We would like to,' I say carefully. 'I hope you would like that too.'

She stares at me a few beats longer.

'Okay,' she says then. Not smiling—but then I wasn't smiling either, and Josie is a serious child.

I take my hand from the wheel, find her little palm and squeeze it. A car honks behind me, and then another. The light is green.

'You know you're my number one, Josie. Always.'

'Yeah,' she says quietly. 'I know.'

The thing is, Josie's smart. I'm sure it's already crossed her mind, what the future might hold for the three of us. After all, she's in the thick of that age when girls get obsessed with fairytales, when Disney princesses are still icons and 'happily ever after' means wedding dresses. It's not that I haven't tried to give her different messaging, of course I have. I want her to be proud of her brains, of her character, of her empathy and resilience and strength. Not of long eyelashes or perfect cuticles. But that's the culture we live in. Josie's seen enough cute-as-a-button stepfamily movies to work out where these things are "supposed" to go.

And she and I are used to being a twosome. She's *used* to having me all to herself, and she's a sensitive child.

After I drop her off I head to the hospital, telling myself it's not a big deal if she didn't jump up and down at the news. That's also something that probably only happens in the movies: real kids need time.

Entering the ICU doesn't feel quite so terrifying as before. I just feel so conspicuous, weirdly aware of my own body, of every squeak of my shoes. This place feels so unnatural. The plastic rings of the privacy curtain slide back and there's Dad—so unlike himself. Dad's five o'clock shadow begins at noon, and when we were kids he used to tease us with his 'scratchy face,' nuzzling our necks until we squealed. Being clean-shaven has always been a point of pride for him. I look down at his grey, scruffed jowls and bite my jaw. Just two nights he's been away from us. It feels like forever.

I brace myself as I reach for his hand. Vaughan

did it so easily, but it doesn't seem natural to me at all. I'm afraid it'll feel cold and lifeless.

But it doesn't. It's warm. Soft and dry and warm. I fold my palm down gently over it, and let it rest there.

I don't know if it's pure imagination—I guess it is—but it's like I can feel him. Like I'm a bird, watching him from overhead as he goes on some solitary journey. I picture him in a desert, walking. A lonely figure.

'Please, Dad,' I whisper. Very quietly, for Dad's ears alone. 'Please, find your way home.'

*

At Bud and Branch, I bury my face in a bowl of peonies. Babette comes in and laughs at me.

'Leave some for the customers, will you, Dinah?'

I don't tell her that this is my medicine, that this is to drive the smell of the hospital away. It almost works. I'm glad to have a place to go that isn't home and isn't the ICU. Vaughan and Lottie weren't sure whether to go into work today, but I knew I had to, just for the sake of keeping going. I sigh, and tie off the latest arrangement with a yellow ribbon.

I haven't told Babette or my co-worker Molly about Dad. I don't want to deal with their sympathy and worried looks. Not yet.

You might have to tell them, Dinah. You might have to, if things get worse and he—

I snap at the voice in my head to be quiet. I can't deal with that right now. Instead I deal with the customers until the bell jangles and I'm left alone once more with my thoughts.

I don't know what my sisters and Mara will say about Max and me. In the middle of everything with Dad…. I just don't want them to think I'm being selfish.

There goes Dinah, stealing the show. Getting engaged while her dad is in the hospital.

Inappropriate.

Hasty.

So dramatic.

I guess the biggest problem is that I just feel disloyal, doing this without Dad. Breaking the news to everyone *but* him.

My phone starts ringing while I'm in the middle of tying an arrangement. Molly's in the back so I have no one to hand off to. My heart's been skittering every time my phone makes a sound, just in case it's Mara or my sisters with news from the hospital. I maneuver the flowers into my left hand and scramble for the phone with my right, and the vase topples and careens across the desk. Luckily Babette's coming out of the back room and somehow just catches it before it goes over the edge.

'Yeow!' She rights it again, her locks still swinging, beads clacking at the ends. 'You think the Patriots are looking for a new quarterback?'

Water's cascading over the edge of the desk, soaking my shoes. I wince.

'Sorry.'

She looks down at my wet shoes and sucks her teeth. 'Those wet feet are what's going to be sorry. Don't go catching a cold now.'

I wait until she's gone into the back office before checking my phone again to make sure the *Sender* bar said what I thought it did.

Jeff McCrae.

I nudge the voicemail alert on the home screen, and listen.

Dinah… I heard the news. I'm real sorry. Gillian told me. I know you must be going through a lot right now but… well, I'm back in town for a bit. I was gonna call you. Gillian's got a casserole she wants to drop off for you folks. Maybe I could come by?

I stare at the screen until it auto-locks and goes black.

Jeff's sister-in-law is great at knowing other people's business, she's been like that since school days. News doesn't sit idle around Gillian McCrae. Of course she's found out about Dad. And *of course* she's told Jeff.

I don't doubt his concern is sincere, but him showing up now… it just feels too disruptive. The thing is, I never *wanted* to push Jeff out of Josie's life. I knew when she and I moved back to Birch Bend it would be harder, but Jeff agreed he'd visit—it might have been the end of him and me, but it wasn't supposed to be the end of him and Josie. But after a year and a half of missed visits, of constantly rescheduled Skype calls, I told him it was better if he just left us to ourselves. Josie was just turning four and I figured she was young enough to adapt. Because my daughter deserved more than some now-and-then attention; more than what was leftover. Josie is incapable of *not* loving people, and it killed me seeing her hold her breath for a card Jeff wouldn't send or a call he wouldn't make. I didn't want her growing up thinking she was worth just the scraps and leftovers of someone's attention. Believe me, I agonized over the decision. But sometimes too little is worse than nothing at all.

And it wasn't like Jeff put up a fight. He was sad and shame-faced but he bowed his head and went along with it. For Josie's sake, he's left us alone.

And most days, I think I made the right choice.

I blink thoughts of Jeff and his family away and stand back to look at the arrangement I'm working on, thread in a few more ferns.

I guess the way some people feel about cats or dogs, I feel about plants. I love how brave they are, how graceful and resourceful; how if you put an obstacle in their way they'll find a way around it. They're humble and, left to themselves, they're strong. And yet in nature they're so vulnerable: there's always someone bigger, clumsier or hungrier, ready to paw them, trample them, pluck them or mangle them.

But despite all that they keep at it, finding ways to thrive, strong and private and silent.

I look at the arrangement again and move one

stem tenderly, just the tiniest sliver to the left. Because sometimes when everything is unbearable, all we have left is beauty.

I sigh.

Yes, I'll call Jeff back. Of course I will.

Just… not yet.

*

'How was school, baby?' I ask as Josie tumbles into the car. I'm picking her up from Trisha's house—she got the bus home with Ashanti earlier. We wave as we back the car out, but once we're on the road Ashanti's loud goodbyes seem to ring in the silence.

'It was okay?' Josie says, turning it into a question.

'Let me guess… you had art class.'

Her hands have splotches of red and green paint on them, and my "detective work" usually makes her giggle. But today she just nods absently, and looks back out the window.

Is it Max? I think.

Or is it Dad?

Dad and Josie have such a wonderful relationship. She's his only grandchild, and even though I thought for a while Vaughan and Mitchell would be producing some more, I suspect they've settled on a no-kids lifestyle for their future. They both travel for work and they both love those high-octane holidays you see advertised in brochures, zip-lining and trekking and all that stuff. So Josie is the only grandchild and the apple of Dad's eye.

I glance in my rearview, make our turn. Josie is

still quiet.

'So do you want to invite Lewis and Ashanti over for your birthday, Jojo?'

That was the plan—not a big birthday party, just her two best friends from school. I checked with Mara if she minded us doing it at the house, and she just gave me that strange vacant look she wears now and said *whatever she wants, Dinah.*

Josie angles her face away from me, out the window. 'Is it okay to have a party?' she says. 'Even though Grandpa's sick?'

My heart aches.

'Grandpa would like to see you having a good time,' I say. And maybe being able to celebrate Josie will give all of us a few hours' respite from the horrible thought-cycle we're all stuck in.

She exhales. I turn into our street.

'Baby?' I say then. 'Do you want to talk about what I said this morning?'

She turns towards me and I can't quite read her expression.

'About Max and me getting married?'

Her eyebrows flare a little like I've said something unexpected, and I think *maybe it wasn't that after all,* but then I see the wave of surprise breaking over my daughter's face, then shock, then glee, and I turn to where her eyes are now fixed.

'It's *Daddy*,' she yelps.

And she's right. It's Jeff's banged-up Buick sitting

on the curb right outside our house, and there, leaning up against it, is Jeff.

Chapter Eight
Lottie

I'm in the attic when I hear voices outside. Looking out the window, I can make out the three figures on the front path, and I hear myself huff in surprise.

Jeff McCrae.

He hasn't been here in *forever*. Last I heard he was off being a grungy-but-successful touring musician somewhere. I feel a flicker of apprehension, seeing him there in the yard. This house used to see a whole lot of Jeff McCrae and it ended in nothing but pain. Now seeing him here for the first time in—what is it, three years?—just makes me expect more disaster. Which is not something our family can afford right now.

I move a little closer to the dormer windows and take in the scene. Josie's practically dancing out there, her little body just about vibrating where she stands. My heart aches for her. This is why Dinah called it, in the end, with Jeff. I know she agonized over the decision, and I know a lot of mothers would have made a different one, but ultimately it was Dinah who asked Jeff to stay out of their lives, given the way his come-and-go (but mostly go) attitude seemed to be affecting Josie. As far as I know he's stayed out of their lives since.

I remember those long-ago days, Dinah flying out the door in her jean jacket, the grin on her face as she hurled herself into the passenger seat in the hand-me-down Nissan Micra Jeff had got from his brother. I kind of resented Jeff for taking her away from me, but I was a little in awe of him too, because he was older, and cool. He didn't make fun of my braces; he smiled at me and stopped to chat. I guess I'm saying Jeff McCrae was never exactly a bad guy. But I guess at some point the rest of us grew up and he didn't. The thing is, good people can hurt you just as bad as bad people, even if they don't mean to.

I watch them out the window, the way Jeff's gesturing, spreading his arms. I crack the window open to hear what's going on. Maybe I shouldn't, but I do. I see Dinah turn to Josie.

'Baby, can you go inside for a minute while I talk to Daddy? Here, take the casserole Gillian made us.' She's got some giant Pyrex dish in her arms.

Casserole? Isn't that for funerals? I feel sick at the thought of who's talking about us in this town, what they're thinking. How maybe they're already forecasting the worst.

'Can't he come in?' Josie says plaintively. I can hear it in her voice, she's certain if she goes inside now she'll lose him, that he'll be gone when she gets back.

'Later, sweetheart,' Dinah says. 'He'll come visit properly soon.'

'Can he come to my birthday party?'

I wince. Dinah said something about having a couple of Josie's friends over tomorrow, and I guess Max will be there too. Adding Jeff to the mix sounds messy. But even from here I can see the way he looks at Dinah when Josie says that, like he really wants to be there.

'We'll talk about it,' Dinah says.

Josie sighs, and slowly turns away from them and trudges up the path. After the door shuts, Jeff starts speaking again.

'Look, Di, I'm sorry I took you by surprise. I just felt so bad when I heard…'

Dinah shakes her head, her voice tight.

'Come on, Jeff. You didn't think I'd be at the house? You didn't consider Josie would be here? And now, of all times? You know you can't just *pop into* Josie's life—do you still not understand what it does to a kid?'

Jeff dips his head but his voice stays firm.

'I hear you, Dinah. I didn't mean to ambush you. But… I've been wanting to talk to you about everything. About Josie.' He looks at her. 'I'm going to be back for a while in Birch Bend and I'm not saying you owe me this, but I'd really like it if we could start doing things differently. With Josie, I mean. If I could be back in her life again. It doesn't really need to be this all-or-nothing, does it?'

Dinah stiffens.

'*You're* the one who made it all-or-nothing, Jeff. Not me.' She sighs. 'You don't get it, Jeff. You just show up like Santa Claus and now she's losing her mind over the fact that you're here. We'd got to a nice, stable place. She was *fine.*'

'Okay.' Jeff nods. 'Okay. I just—'

'You've forced my hand, Jeff,' she interrupts. 'Josie knows you're here now, and I can't just forbid her to see you. I'm not going to. But here's the thing: if the most she can expect after this summer is a video call every six months, don't shower her with attention now. It'll be like dropping off a cliff for her.'

There's silence, and I think it's the silence of Jeff swallowing his pride, wanting to defend himself but choosing not to.

Maybe he *has* done some growing up these past few years.

'I don't want that either,' he says finally. 'Truly.'

There's a beat, and then she nods—a short, sharp flick of her head.

'I guess I'll call you tomorrow then. It won't be much of a party, but we'll see you around five.'

They stand there a moment, looking at each other. The magnolia tree quivers in a gust behind them, like it too is exhaling. Jeff turns and goes off down the path, and I watch Dinah linger for a moment before she heads this way.

So that's it. Jeff McCrae is back in town. I wonder what Dad would say about that.

I pull back from the window, accidentally knocking a box at my feet, and hold back a sneeze as dust motes rise into the air. One of the Bonnie boxes.

There's a stash of them up here. Not the valuable stuff—that went to Vaughan and Dinah years ago—but trinkets and sentimental items. It sounds like Bonnie was a real hoarder. Mom says she kept every birthday card, every postcard she'd ever received, and Dad had to throw out bags upon bags of stuff in the months after she died.

I can't imagine what it would be like to have to go through that.

I say a prayer that we're not about to find out.

Just thinking about it takes me back to this morning, and the weird thing that happened right after I went to visit Dad. I'd decided to go into work for the day just to give my brain something else to think about, but figured I'd call by Dad's garage on the way. It turned out nobody had thought to tell Casey—the guy that's been helping Dad out in the garage the past eight months or so—anything about what happened. We didn't even have his number. So I just took the keys and drove over, figuring I'd catch him there.

But when I arrived there was no Casey, and when I unlocked the door and went in, the place was empty. Clean. Not a car in sight. Daddy usually has three or four in there at once, in various stages of repair. But now there were none. And there was something about the place, how tidy it looked. Vacant.

Just call Casey, I told myself, figuring he'd have answers.

I went into the back office, found the address book

Dad keeps by the landline—he loves his smartphone but his hands get greasy at work. Casey's name was right there on the inside cover.

He picked up right away, sounding startled.

'George?' His voice was so surprised, I thought at first maybe he already knew about Dad. But when I introduced myself and explained he was in hospital, there was just this pause, and then a confused, polite voice.

'Hey Lottie. I'm really sorry about your dad. I hope he bounces back soon. But ya know, I haven't worked out there for over a month now.'

I didn't get it. I still don't. Why would Dad have let him go? And why not tell us? Casey stayed on the line a little longer, sounding as confused as I was. He said Dad had just told him he didn't have need of the help anymore.

'I'm not complaining, he was pretty decent about it. But if something needs doing at the shop, sorry, I can't help you. Got a new gig last week.'

I put down the phone and stared around at the empty garage floor. I didn't go to work after that—I knew there wasn't a chance in hell I would be able to focus.

I don't know if I should tell Mom about it all. She's just been so out of it since everything happened. Half the time she's in Stepford mode, and the other half she just seems lost. I don't know if she can take anything more to worry about. Meanwhile, I've no idea why Dad would have let Casey go but the only thing I can think of is that the business has been doing badly. I just never thought Dad would keep a thing like that from us.

Maybe, the voice inside me says. *Maybe he would if it was really, really bad.*

I sigh, and close the attic door behind me.

*

'Did Josie come in here?' I say, and Mom looks up from the stove and nods. She's making a vegetable lasagna—she's in Stepford mode right now, I guess.

'About ten minutes ago,' Mom says. 'Apparently, Jeff McCrae's back.'

I can hear it in her voice, the tone that says *just what we need right now*, and I can't help but agree.

'I saw,' I nod.

Mom looks back at the saucepan. 'I drove past his mother's house the other day. It's up for sale. I'm betting that's why he's in town.'

'I think Josie's pretty excited he's back,' I say.

'I think so too,' Mom sighs. She rests the wooden spoon against the pot and we slip into silence.

'Can I help?' I say.

'No help necessary, Lottie.' Mom switches to that bright, brittle voice again, and I know my attempt at real conversation is over. Part of me wants to put my arms around her and tell her to let it all out, snap out of this fake *I'm-fine* mode she's in these days. But then again, maybe that's what's *keeping* her from snapping.

'Was that Jeff McCrae outside?' Vaughan comes

into the kitchen. I notice again the big dark circles under her eyes. They were bad when she got here, even before everything with Dad—I remember thinking that when she drove up on Friday night. That's already unusual for Vaughan. Now they're ten times worse.

'Yes.' Dinah's voice is crisp as she enters the room. I guess she overheard Vaughan on the stairs. 'As you all seem to have noticed, Jeff is back in Birch Bend for a little while.' She frowns at the table where Gillian McCrae's casserole is sitting. 'His mom's got a buyer for the house, so he's helping his brother clear the place out.'

'So?' Vaughan says gently. 'How was the conversation?'

Dinah scowls.

'Well, he took us by surprise. Josie…' She sighs. 'I guess she misses him.'

There's a beat.

'He's still her father,' Vaughan offers. Vaughan's the only one who can afford to say things like that to Dinah. Mom and I wouldn't dare.

Dinah winces.

'He said he'd like things to be different, to try harder. I can't say I'm convinced but I can't just tell him to go away, not when he's already shown up on the doorstep and Josie's all hyped about it.' She shrugs tiredly. 'She's not three years old anymore. If I take this away from her now we'll never get past it.'

'Well,' Vaughan says slowly. 'Three years is a while. People can change. Maybe it's a good thing you're giving him another shot.'

Dinah nods, then sinks into one of the kitchen chairs. She pushes the Pyrex dish away from her. Then she looks around at us and clears her throat.

'While we're here,' she says, and suddenly her voice doesn't sound tired anymore. 'There's... something I want to tell you.' She stops. I feel the little pause, the way Mom and Vaughan and I all get a little stiller.

'I'm going to marry Max,' she says. 'He asked me to marry him.'

Mom's spoon falls fully into the pot this time, with a clunk.

'Congratulations,' Vaughan says finally.

'Congratulations.' I clear my throat. 'It's, um, great news.'

I don't dislike Max. But they haven't been together all that long, and I guess he's just not the type of guy I'd have pictured for Dinah.

'We needed a piece of good news around here,' Vaughan says gently.

Mom has her back to us all, like she suddenly can't bear to take her eyes off the lasagna.

'I... I'm sorry,' she says finally. 'I'm glad you're happy, Dinah. But I don't think I can celebrate anything right now.'

She leaves the kitchen without even turning off the stove. I look at Vaughan, who looks at Dinah. Dinah scowls at Gillian McCrae's casserole.

'It *is* good news,' she says. 'And nobody can take that away from us.'

Then she leaves too. Vaughan and I look at each other, and Vaughan turns off the stove. I guess we'll all be eating separately tonight.

George

George is beginning to get used to the darkness now. It's like being in a forest at night... only he can't remember where he started walking from, or where he's supposed to be going.

Does it matter? A voice seems to say. It sounds familiar somehow. A voice he knew long ago.

You're here now, it says. *There's no hurry, Georgie. Not any more.*

Maybe the voice is right, George thinks. Maybe he should just... relax. Let go. Maybe he should ignore that other voice at the back of his mind, telling him there's something he's forgotten; something he needs to go back for.

Go back? The new voice says, almost like it's teasing him. *Go back* where, *George?*

And George can't quite seem to remember

Chapter Nine
Dinah

I have to haul myself out of deep sleep to reach for the alarm clock. I'm so groggy, my dreams are still trailing around me like a fog. But Dad was there, I know that much. I blink up at the ceiling, trying to anchor myself in reality again, this new reality that I wish so hard we weren't all living in. Waking up's the worst part, I've decided. That feeling before it sinks in, when you're groping to remember what's happened, knowing that it's bad but not quite remembering—and then it hits you like a kick in the teeth. I turn off the alarm and lay a moment listening to the church on Suffolk Street chime the hour, thinking of those times Daddy would take us to church, even though he isn't exactly a regular. He mainly liked to go for the music. I remember him once gesturing backwards towards the organ: *That's where the God is, Dinah*, he told me, pointing with his thumb. *In the music. That's where you find it.*

I look over at Josie on the twin bed by the window. She's got her arms wrapped around Pig, the favorite stuffed animal that she recently told me she had outgrown and was giving up. I packed him anyway, and I'm glad I did. But it kills me to see it, how small and vulnerable she looks despite trying so hard to be grown up.

I hadn't planned to make that announcement last night. I look down at my hand where the ring sits—I put it on last night when I came upstairs. And that's where it's going to stay.

'Jo-bear.' I squeeze her shoulder under the covers. 'Time for school.'

Josie wriggles away from my hand, burrowing into warm sheets, but I guess my voice must find its way to her sleeping thoughts all the same because she swivels around then, her eyes popping open.

'Mommy! I was dreaming about Grandpa.'

Me too, I don't say. I don't want her to know that I'm just a child too right now—afraid like she is, uncertain like she is.

'I miss him,' she says. 'I want him to come home.'

This time I don't hesitate to say it.

'Me too, baby. Me too.'

I make her breakfast downstairs. The house is quiet.

'Is Daddy going to visit Grandpa in the hospital too?' Josie says as she chews.

I swallow.

'I don't think your dad will be visiting Grandpa,' I say slowly. 'It's immediate family only. The part of the hospital he's in right now, everyone has to work very hard. They don't want a lot of visitors getting in their way.'

She pushes her juice glass back and forth on the table, making rings. 'If there are too many visitors what happens?' she says.

'We just want to help all the nurses and doctors to do their job,' I say.

'So people don't die?' She looks up at me.

'Oh, sweetheart,' I say.

She looks out the window.

Josie and I talked a lot about Jeff last night. I made sure she understood that Jeff was only home for a little while, maybe not even for the full summer. Just long enough to help his brother clear out the house and sell up, I explained.

'How long do houses take to sell?' she'd asked. It breaks my heart how transparent it is.

'And then he'll go back to New York City?' she'd said, like it was a faraway country.

I think I'll ask Jeff if he wants to come over before the party starts. I need to give Josie some time alone with him. Maybe it's not a bad thing he's coming: he and Max will have to meet sometime, I guess, and a few extra people in the room might make it easier.

I wonder what Max will think when I tell him Jeff's back in town.

Josie and I haven't been in the habit of talking about her father much, not any more. I felt Josie had adjusted pretty nicely to us being a single-parent family. And maybe she had, but seeing Jeff appear yesterday like some sort of mirage seems to have wiped away whatever work I thought I'd done.

I drain the coffee from my mug and pour some more from the jug. Josie looks at me dubiously.

'I think Pig might be getting sick,' she says.

I give her my best smile.

'Well then, I'll take extra good care of him while you're at school today.'

'What if he needs me to stay home and take care of him?'

I take her plate to the sink.

'Pig is so strong, baby. I think he would want you to go to school.' I look over my shoulder. 'But if you want, we can put him in your backpack and you can take him with you?'

She flushes, no doubt thinking that almost-seven is too old for a stuffed animal.

'That's okay,' she sighs.

'I'm calling Lewis and Ashanti's moms about your party, okay?' I say.

'And Daddy,' she says.

I sigh inwardly.

'And Jeff.'

I hoist her backpack from the hall and she shunts her arms into it, frowning like she's preparing for war.

'Noble girl.' I plant a kiss on her scalp and she wrinkles her nose.

*

Once I drop Josie off I step on the gas and make my way to the hospital.

Dad lies still as a log. His stubble has grown out further and it makes me feel sick, like I'm watching nature take him back.

Can you hear us, Daddy? Can he feel that I'm here? I wonder where his mind is right now, if he feels trapped or peaceful.

It was Dad who suggested Josie and I move back in with him and Lottie and Mara for our first couple of months back in Birch Bend. He was the one who fell in love with Josie so much that we didn't leave for six months. From the moment she was born Dad adored Josie. He loved having us to say, didn't mind that she was teething and a terrible sleeper; that she sometimes woke the house up wailing multiple times a night. He didn't talk about how Lottie was in the middle of her college applications like Mara did, as though my poor choices were getting in the way of Lottie's future.

It was Dad who came apartment-hunting with me, Josie riding tall on his shoulders and giggling, and who helped pay our rent those first months when we moved into our own place and it was taking me a while to get back on my feet. He worked late at the garage, taking on extra projects and side-jobs to make sure we always had enough. He was the one who watched Josie two afternoons a week to cut down my childcare bills, and made it sound like it was the greatest privilege of his life, not a burden of bottles and dirty diapers.

Now I listen to the machines breathing and pulsing around him. They sound louder than before, although maybe that's my imagination too. They seem deafening, a terrible mechanical chorus.

You can do it, I think at him. *You can beat this thing, I know you can.* I close my eyes and for a moment I feel him in the room—not where his body is, but all around.

I'm trying, his voice seems to say.

I blink my eyes open, breathing fast. Was it just my imagination; just the effect of too much desperate hope?

When it's time to go I squeeze his hand, papery-dry but still the same: his piano-player hands, heavy and deft and strong.

'See you soon,' I say. *See you soon,* like a prayer.

I breathe in deep in the parking lot as soon as I'm back outside.

Molly waves at me as I step into Bud and Branch and unsling my bag.

'Woah! *Dinah!*' She's suddenly wide-eyed, beaming. I follow her gaze and see the engagement ring glinting on my finger.

'Oh. Yeah, um. Max and I are getting married.'

'That's *huge,* oh my gosh, *congratulations*!' Molly bounds at me with a hug. I feel bad that I can barely hug back. But if I let myself lean into it I think I might come completely undone, and that's not what people want from a bride-to-be.

'So?' She draws out the word, waiting for more. 'When? Where? Is Josie so psyched?'

I feel a pang of guilt.

'You know, it's kind of a weird time right now,' I say. 'My dad's not doing so well, so we're putting a lot of the details on hold.'

Not doing so well is the understatement of the century, but Molly must grasp more than I'm saying because her face absolutely falls.

'Oh man.' She squeezes my shoulder. 'I'm so sorry, Dinah. I had no idea.'

'Thanks,' I say awkwardly.

The shop bell rings, and I turn to see Gillian McCrae walk in. *Great.* Jeff's sister-in-law is hardly a regular at Bud and Branch and I'm pretty sure she's not here for the tulips. Some people just have a morbid curiosity to hear about other people's misfortunes.

'Gillian,' I say. 'How are you?'

'How are *you,* more like? And your poor family?' She shakes her head, and I flush.

'Well, we've been better.'

'Is he going to be okay, do you think?'

She actually sounds genuinely concerned. I meet her eyes and for a moment there's a flash of something between us, like we're really seeing each other. I blink and look away. My skin prickles. I'm not used to this feeling. Not from Gillian McCrae, anyway, or Gillian Holland as she was back in high school. I never thought she liked me much.

'I… we don't know.' I swallow to make sure my voice doesn't give way. 'They say we still have every reason to hope.'

The frown on her face deepens a little. *Every reason to hope.* We both know what's behind that tired line.

But she nods then, slowly.

'Hope is good, Dinah. None of us get far without it.'

I feel the welling behind my eyes and push myself to smile. Gillian McCrae has never made me smile, much less cry. Until now.

'And I'll, um take this,' she says, taking an orchid from the display and putting it on the counter.

I swallow and ring her up.

'Tell them all I'm praying for them,' she says.

'I will,' I say quietly as she leaves.

*

It's barely lunch time when I get the call from Josie's school.

She's at the nurse's office apparently. She doesn't feel well, she wants to go home.

Oh, Josie-bear.

'I don't want to presume, Ms. Spencer,' the secretary says. 'But her teacher mentioned you're dealing with a family illness right now. It might be more of, well, an emotional thing.'

I'm pretty sure that's true. Josie's emotionally delicate, but physically sturdy. I doubt she came down with something since I dropped her off at school today.

'Can I speak to her?' I say.

When they put her on the phone, she's quiet.

'Baby, what's wrong?'

'I… have a tummy-ache,' she says, in the small voice that tells me for sure the 'tummy-ache' doesn't exist. The ache is something different. I sigh, but don't let her hear it.

Babette is going to hate this.

'Okay, sweetheart. Just sit tight a little longer, okay? I'm coming to get you right now.'

*

Nobody's home when we get back to the house—I guess whoever hasn't gone to work must be at the hospital. I tuck Josie into bed and bring her some broth and toast. Even a phantom stomachache can benefit from comfort food.

'Feeling better?' I say, when she hands me back the half-drunk broth.

'Did you tell Daddy I'm sick?' she says.

I put the broth down on the floor.

'No, I didn't. Do you want me to tell him to come by?' I say carefully.

She nods.

I hesitate. 'If you want to see him, of course I'll ask him to come. But you know you don't have to be sick for me to call him, right?'

She drops her eyes.

'Yeah. I know.'

Maybe this is for the best, I tell myself as I pick up the phone—my work day's a write-off anyway and I need to have a calm conversation with Jeff at some stage. Josie's birthday party won't be the time or place.

When he picks up I'm prepared for him to act awkward or make excuses, but he doesn't.

'I'm glad she wants to see me,' he says, and pauses. 'Thanks for letting me come by.'

I hold my tongue rather than remind him this is a privilege I'm hoping not to regret .

'Also,' I say. 'We should talk. If you really want to be back in Josie's life, I mean—we should talk about what that looks like.'

'I'd like that,' Jeff says, somewhat to my surprise.

I check on Josie after I put down the phone, and tidy a few things around the house while I wait. I'm in the living room when I spot movement on the front path. I open the door before he gets to it, his hand still extended for the bell.

'Oh,' he says, dropping his arm. 'Hi.'

It's that trademark smile that the moms of Birch Bend always used to be so charmed by. Charm was never Jeff's problem. But is it my wishful thinking that there's something different in that smile now—something a little older, a little sadder; a little more serious?

In his other hand he's holding a stuffed turtle with a ribbon around it.

'Cute.' I nod. 'You didn't have to.'

'Does she still like turtles?' he says, and I nod. Turtles were three-year-old Josie's obsession.

I bring him upstairs, explaining about the "stomachache". He looks at me with an expression of utter sincerity.

'I'm so sorry for what you're all going through, Di.'

He's a good guy, I remind myself. Bad at follow-through, bad at taking responsibility, but his heart is soft. Maybe too soft.

'Daddy!' Josie says when he walks in. I try to feel only good things at how her face lights up on seeing him.

'I'll leave you two to chat.' I head back downstairs, feeling the beginnings of a headache. Maybe I shouldn't dismiss Josie's stomachache as a phantom pain—stress can do all sorts of things to you.

It was a cliché, wasn't it, falling for a musician? The thing is, Jeff really did have an extraordinary gift. It was half of what I loved in him, and it was also what made our lives together impossible. Normal teen talent—football, gymnastics—maybe it snags you some medals or an edge in your college applications, and then it fades away. But Jeff... he had the kind of talent that claims you, the kind you can't let go of. So I guess he had to let go of something, and it was us.

I could have seen it coming, though. I *did* see it coming. When I told him I was pregnant he bought me a cheap ring and alcohol-free cider to toast the occasion, and I told myself everything would still be perfect, that we were just going through a rough patch. That if I never spoke about what I knew, I could heal. *We* could heal.

But that's a fool's logic.

Still, I'll give Jeff this: together we made a miracle.

I turn on the water and tackle the saucepans

someone's left to soak in the sink since this morning. My thoughts go back to Dad, to the balloon pump coaxing his heart along and how much I resent it, that horrible, horribly necessary pump. I want to take the saucepans out of the sink and smash them against something. Instead I sponge each one carefully, delicately, and set it to dry.

I startle when Jeff's voice sounds behind me.

'She really is an amazing kid.'

I turn. He's standing by the kitchen table, hands on the back of a dining chair, keeping a polite distance. I see his eyes traveling around the kitchen—this kitchen that has changed so little in the years since he's been here.

I look at him. 'Yeah, she really is.' *And she's what you walked away from,* I don't say.

'So, no word on your dad?' he says, and I shake my head.

'They're waiting for his heart function to improve before they take him out of sedation.' I say it like it's something that *will* happen, not just something that might. I hope I sound more confident than I feel.

There's a sympathetic silence, and after a while my nerves start jangling. I plunge my hands back in the soapy water, glad to find a caked-on bit of grease to scrub.

'Hey,' Jeff says after a while. 'Gillian mentioned… you and Max Brannagh?'

Jeff's sister-in-law has a way of knowing just about everyone in this town. I know she's involved with

CLAIRE AMARTI

the local library and its fund drives. Alane Brannagh's heavily involved with those too. That's probably how Gillian got her intel.

I let the water out of the sink before turning around. The diamond winks at me through a bubble of soap-suds. It's awkward, meeting Jeff's eyes. The past is the past, but right now it's in the room with us.

'That's right.' I clear my throat. 'We're, um, we're engaged, actually.'

'You're... wow.' Jeff's smile doesn't falter. 'Congratulations, Dinah.'

I fold the dish-towel, mainly so I can have something to do with my hands.

'Thank you. It's all come at kind of a weird time, but...'

I trail off, and Jeff nods.

'And you?' I say, unsure if I should ask. 'I mean... anyone special these days?'

The question doesn't land like I thought it would. Jeff's face shifts.

'Oh. You didn't hear?'

I shake my head, wondering what I'm supposed to have heard. I don't really do Facebook, and we don't exactly have mutual friends these days.

Jeff looks at the floor, expels a quick breath.

'Sorry, I just—I figured you'd have heard. I was with someone, until last year. She got sick.' He takes a deep breath. 'I mean, I guess she was sick when I met her. But she was strong. She beat it the first

102

time.'

I feel a wave of shock, then sympathy, as I process what he's telling me. That kind of tragedy is not for people like Jeff. Light-hearted, chilled-out Jeff…

'Oh, Jeff. I'm so sorry. I had no idea…'

He nods. I don't know what to say. I guess I did have the feeling something had changed in him, but I never imagined it was something like this. I feel so guilty for seeing him in the same light I had for years: flaky Jeff, barely-there Jeff. Like he wasn't capable of being hurt.

'I'm so sorry,' I repeat.

He gives me a pained smile.

'It's life, I guess. Sometimes the gifts we're given aren't given for very long.'

This strikes me as an unbearably generous way of looking at it, and a lump comes to my throat. If Daddy doesn't come back to us… will I ever be able to find that kind of acceptance and grace?

Jeff stands there, and I stand with the dish-cloth still in my hands, and I don't know what else to say. Then comes the sound of a car outside, and it's like we both wake up.

The car door slams, and through the leaves of the magnolia I see Max walking up the driveway. He sees me at the window, a half-smile ebbing as his eyes travel to the other figure in the room. I don't know how well he can see Jeff from there, and I don't know that he'd recognize him anyway. Max mostly knows Jeff by reputation, through me, and it's hardly been a glowing account. I'm just wishing I'd had the time to brief him on Jeff's re-appearance.

'Well, look at that for timing,' I say.

I swing the door open as Max walks up.

'Max! I didn't know you were coming.'

He's got a big pizza box in one hand.

'I texted you a bunch of times,' he says, and I remember that I left my phone in my bag, hanging at the foot of the stairs.

'I just wanted to check on you,' he continues. 'I thought I could bring you dinner.' He nods at the pizza box and I see it's from his restaurant. Little B's does great pizza.

'I see you have company,' he says

Jeff has followed me to the doorway, hovering a few feet back. I clear my throat.

'Um, yes. Max, this is Jeff. Josie's dad. Jeff, Max.'

There's a pause.

'Glad to meet you,' Jeff says. 'Congratulations on the engagement.'

'Thanks,' Max says, giving me a slightly disguised *what the hell* look.

'Jeff is just back in town for a little while,' I say. 'His mom's house is being sold. We're'—I shoot Jeff a look—'just talking about how to handle things in a way that's good for Josie.'

Jeff nods awkwardly.

'Well, I certainly hope I'm not interrupting,' Max says crisply. I put my hand on his arm and give it a little squeeze in a way that I hope says *of course not* but also, *be nice.*

'I was just leaving,' Jeff says. 'So, um, see you soon.'

'I'll text you about the birthday thing,' I say, and he nods.

And then he's gone. Max looks at me.

'Well, that was a trip. Since when is *he* back?'

I shrug. 'A couple of days? He... he seems to really want to be a part of Josie's life again.'

'And you're going to let him?' Max looks skeptical. Which isn't surprising, given what I've told him.

I sigh, shutting the door behind us and taking the pizza from him.

'I'm not exactly happy about it, but Josie has a mind of her own these days. I could make decisions for her when she was three, but... well, she really wants to see him, Max, and he wants to see her.'

Max frowns.

'I felt like I was walking into something... I don't know.' His frown grows as he looks at me. 'You looked so deep in conversation when I saw you through the window.' He pauses. 'I thought you and Jeff didn't get on.'

I shrug.

'We do and we don't, I guess,' I say. 'It's the "don't" part that matters.'

*

I take a slice of the pizza and leave the rest on the table for the others. Max heads home, making me promise to keep my phone on me tomorrow.

'I was worried,' he says. I want to tell him not to be, but then, I'm worried too.

I get Josie ready for bed early. She really does seem tired.

'It's good that Daddy's back for the summer, isn't it?' She looks up at me. 'So he can take care of me if you have to take care of Grandpa.'

I feel a pang.

'I'll always, *always* take care of you. You know that.' I sweep the hair back from her face.

'It's nice that your dad is going to be around for a little bit,' I say, trying to keep my voice neutral. 'But you remember what we talked about last night, right? That he's going away again in a while, and your daddy has a hard time staying as organized as he wants to be… and how it might be hard for him to keep in touch so much when he goes back to the city.'

'Why would it be hard?' she says, a hint of mutiny in her voice.

I hold in the sigh.

You better not mess this up, Jeff.

'Sometimes other people are very different from us,' I say finally. 'And what's easy for us is hard for them.'

She's silent for a while, long enough that I think her thoughts have moved on. But then, 'Is that why you and Grandma aren't friends?' she says.

I feel a wash of shame.

'What do you mean, baby?'

106

Grandma means Mara, of course. For all the baggage between Mara and me, I think Mara deserves that—she's been there through Josie's whole life and I know how much she loves her. But it hurts sometimes, knowing that there's someone else that name is really meant for. A person Josie will never get to meet.

'Is that why you and Grandma aren't friends,' Josie repeats. 'Because she's very different from you?'

I pick up a gnawed crust that's fallen on the duvet. I've never wanted Josie to feel pulled in two directions—that's why I've tried never to badmouth her dad in front of her, though I've been tempted. And it's why I never want her to see tension between me and the grandma she loves.

'Sweetheart, it's not that Mara and I aren't friends.' I hesitate. 'It's just… you're right, she and I are very different people. And when two people are very different sometimes they have trouble understanding each other. Sometimes they get frustrated.'

Josie squints as she evaluates me.

'And Aunt Lottie?' she says.

I blink.

'What about Aunt Lottie?'

'Are you very different from her too? Because sometimes you seem really mad at her.'

I wince. I'm so lucky that my daughter is this beautiful, perceptive little creature. But sometimes I wish she were just a little less perceptive.

There was a time when I would have said Lottie and I weren't that different.

There was a time when I would have said those differences didn't matter.

But that was then and this is now.

'We are, honey-bunch,' I say. 'We're very different people.'

Josie frowns, tucking Pig deeper in the crook of her elbow.

'But you're *sisters*,' she says. I think of the sisters in the Narnia books she loves so much: Lucy the baby, and Susan the big sister, the protector. I nod, and don't correct her with *half-sisters*, because degrees of blood aren't what matters here. They never have been. But how do I explain to a child that sometimes in this house, this beautiful house where we grew up wanting for nothing, sometimes it feels like there isn't quite enough to go around? I pull Josie in close and kiss her head. It smells warm and dry, like a sun-warmed chick. And to hide the lump in my throat I have to turn away. Because right now, her insistence—*family, family, above all, family*—reminds me of no one so much as her grandpa. And tonight my biggest fear is that she won't get to grow up knowing him.

Then out the window I see Lottie walking up the drive. I watch her slump-shouldered walk, nesting my chin on the top of Josie's warm head.

I remember Lottie at twelve, thirteen. How she used to tell me about anything bad that happened to her at school; how when she got her period she locked herself in the bathroom and wouldn't let anyone in. Not Mara, not Vaughan. *Only Dinah*, she'd yelled through the door.

Now I have a sister I hardly speak to.

And a father who may never speak again.

We're a family fraying at the seams. One good tug could tear the stitches right out.

Chapter Ten
Lottie

I close the front door quietly.

Going to work today wasn't easy. My boss had evidently told the team about Dad, probably to make it easier on me, which meant I mainly spent the day assuring people how fine I was, or dodging sympathetic faces. That, and Googling medical terms. It's so hard to imagine tomorrow, and so easy to imagine yesterday. But the clocks keep ticking forwards, bringing us further and further into this wrong future.

But the weirdest part of my day was when I swung by the hospital after work. One of the machines hooked up to Dad had started chirping and I'd been looking around frantically, panicked that nobody was moving to help. When a nurse finally showed up he told me it was just an alert to change the IV, and I guess I must have looked pretty frantic because he started chatting to me, nodding at Dad and asking if I was his daughter.

I'd nodded.

'Lottie,' I'd said.

He gave me a gentle smile.

'Ah,' he said. 'I thought maybe you were Bonnie.'

I blinked at him, and must have stuttered

something that made him repeat it..

'He mentioned a Bonnie.' The nurse shrugged. 'When he arrived. He was conscious for a little bit, in and out, before he went to surgery.'

'He was?'

The nurse nodded.

'He was pretty out of it.'

I felt winded.

'And he said *Bonnie*?'

His eyes crinkled in concern. 'I'm sorry. I didn't mean to distress you.'

I just stood there for a moment.

Bonnie?

Maybe it was stupid, but I just felt this *rage*. *We* were the ones left behind. Why wasn't he saying our names? When the nurse left again and I was alone with Dad, I couldn't help the panicky flutter in my chest. It was as though I could *feel* her in the air; as though there was a thread she was tugging on, pulling him away from us and back to her. Reclaiming what had been hers.

Give him back, I thought in a silent fury.

Stupid, maybe, but I couldn't shake it and still can't—this idea that she's fighting us somehow. As if she's over there on the opposite shore, and Dad's in the middle of some terrible tug of war. Standing by his bed, I had this horrible fear that she would win.

Maybe that's why I find myself dumping my things in my room and heading up to the attic, pulling the "Bonnie box" I tripped on yesterday out

111

from the wall and lifting the lid. I don't know what I'm hoping to find, exactly. Maybe I just want to remind myself that she's gone and that she was only ever human-sized, not some larger-than-life, faceless ghost.

It's a sea of memories in there. I guess Mom wasn't kidding about Bonnie being a packrat. Movie stubs, birthday cards, champagne corks with things written on them like *Sarah's 30th!* A Magic 8-Ball. A china doll, face-down on a stash of magazine clippings. I fish out a Kodak packet of photos.

What strikes me first is how much Dinah has grown to look like her mom. The second thing that strikes me is how young Bonnie was—probably just Dinah's age now when she had the accident.

Everyone gets younger as I flick backwards. There are pictures of toddler Vaughan and baby Dinah. A birthday party, tots in paper-cone hats, Bonnie leaning over the table, laughing.

Bonnie at Christmas, Dinah on her lap.

Bonnie at a fairground, smiling.

Bonnie under a tree in the sun.

There are pictures of her and Dad, too. There's a look in his eyes that just hits me right in the chest. He's looking at Bonnie and it's this look of frank adoration, like he hardly dares breathe in case he wakes up and finds her gone. He loves Mom, I know he does, but I've never seen him look at her like *that*. It plays in a loop in my mind, the nurse's words from earlier. How can Bonnie ever really be gone when we're all living in *her* house, eating at the table she chose, sitting in the armchairs she bought, sleeping in the rooms *she* slept in?

I dust my hand over the china doll and set it upright. I bet it was bought to look like Bonnie as a child. Her genes have come down the line so strongly, though, that it might as well have been bought to resemble Josie—those big brown eyes, the wild cloud of hair. It's a beautiful doll, and I put it aside before I close the box. Josie might like it.

I see the headlights of Mom's car in the driveway as I press the lid down tight. Whatever I thought this would bring me—comfort? Closure?—it isn't. I feel a bit dirty, trespassing like this in someone else's memories.

Down in my room, I sit the doll on my bookshelf for now. Maybe I can ask Vaughan what she thinks. I'm not about to tell Dinah I've been snooping in her mom's old things. The doll looks back at me, glassy eyes staring. Her head's on a tilt, giving her a quizzical look.

I pass Vaughan's room on the way downstairs. She's on the phone and her voice is raised, agitated. Everything about Vaughan always seems so well-managed and seamless. I wonder if it's Mitchell she's talking to; I've never really pictured them fighting.

A hollow feeling creeps in my stomach. I have... complicated feelings about their relationship. Still, Vaughan has always seemed happy in her marriage.

And that's a good thing, I remind myself.

Mom's at the kitchen table, staring out the window.

'How was Dad?' I say, and she startles.

She starts, then turns. 'Not much change.' She looks at me. 'It doesn't sound like they're seeing the kind of improvement they'd like, Lottie.'

I feel winded. It's not *news*… but it's the first time any of us have dared to say this out loud.

'What about the pump?' I say feebly.

Mom shrugs. 'It's doing its job. But it's not long term, Lottie.'

I take a breath. I know it's true; of course I know it. The pump is temporary. Just something to buy us a little time so Dad's heart can get back up to speed. But that's not happening.

Yet, I remind myself. It's not happening *yet.*

We sit in silence for a while.

'Mom?' I say finally.

She nods.

'I was up in the attic just now…' I hesitate. 'You know those boxes of Bonnie's?'

She nods, frowning.

'I was just…'—suddenly I don't want to admit I was rifling through them—'…thinking about them. About her. You know, I've never really heard much about what happened to Bonnie.'

Mom looks at me.

'Of course you know what happened.'

'No, I mean…' I swallow. 'The accident: I don't

know about it. I mean… where did it happen? Where was Dad when he found out? Was it… did she die instantly?'

Suddenly it feels unthinkable that I don't know the details. It's a moment that has shaped all our lives and I have no idea what it was like.

Mom sighs.

'He was at home with the girls; they were asleep. Police officers came for him, brought him out to identify her.' She pauses. 'He knocked on my door, frantic. I went next door and stayed in the house with the girls until he came back.'

I hadn't known that part. They'd been neighbors; maybe even friends. But I didn't know Mom had been involved on that actual night.

'Some driver had called it in,' she goes on, in a detached, faraway voice. 'There were no witnesses to the actual crash, but she was dead when the ambulance arrived.' Mom pauses. 'It was in Barksville, I gather.'

'What was she doing out there?' Barksville's a community near Birch Bend that's fancier than most, full of big houses set far apart, and lush lawns with sprinklers.

Mom shrugs.

'I think she was just out for a spin. Your dad said she used to do that sort of thing—just get in the car for a while to clear her head.' She examines her hands. 'My mother used to do that too, back when. I suppose there wasn't much you could do for therapy in her day—it was either that or booze. No Xanax, back then,' she adds wryly.

Funny, Mom never talks about her mother—it's just one of the things she's typically so private about. Even though she's an only child, they're not close.

She looks at me then.

'This is something I wouldn't say to your sisters. But I think Bonnie found being at home claustrophobic sometimes. She married very young, you know.'

I've always pictured Bonnie as someone infatuated with her life: devoted wife, adoring mother.

'It just seems so random,' I say. If Bonnie hadn't been on that particular road that particular night... I wouldn't even exist.

'Yes.' Mom's eyes drift to the window. 'Tragedy is like that. I know your father went through a period, too, of wondering. Why that road. Why that hour. Why that moment.' She pauses. 'I think sometimes we just find it easier to say there must have been a reason, you know? To tell ourselves there's a story behind everything. We look for the smaller answers because we know in our hearts we'll never get the big answer—the one we really need.'

We're silent then for a moment. When she turns back from the window her eyes look so tired.

'Lottie?'

I nod.

'Did your father... say anything to you? The day of the party. Before... you know.'

I frown. 'You mean the announcement?' I ask. 'The thing he was about to say?'

'Yes.' Mom looks away from me. 'I just can't stop wondering,' she says. 'I can't stop asking myself what was on his mind.'

*

I wake up sweating in the middle of the night. The moon's coming bright through the window. I was having a nightmare. It fades as soon as I open my eyes but the feeling of it lingers around me, tainting everything with darkness. My room doesn't look like it usually does. The ceilings seem to hide shadows; the walls watch me.

I had nightmares a lot as a child. Dinah was the one whose bed I snuck into on those nights when I woke up breathless with fright. She'd pull the covers back without quite opening her eyes, and wrap one arm around me.

I sit up in bed and let the sweat on my neck grow cool.

I'm thinking of Bonnie again. Of Daddy calling out her name. Of the way she sometimes seems to own this house at night.

The clock ticks quietly. I push back the sheet and put my feet down on cool floorboards. They creak as I pad to the window, where moonlight cuts a swathe across my body. Bits of the nightmare are coming back to me now. I was trapped somewhere—one of those lucid dreams where you know you're asleep but can't wake up.

Is that how Dad feels right now? Trapped and unable to wake up?

I look over at Bonnie's doll, glassy-eyed on the shelf. She stares back at me.

What will happen to us? I ask silently.

But the doll just stares and keeps her secrets.

I think about what Mom said earlier, about how we keep ourselves distracted by looking for the answers that don't matter. And maybe she's right.

But maybe if we knew the right questions to ask, we wouldn't even dare. Maybe we'd be too scared of where the answers would lead us.

Chapter Eleven
Dinah

I wake with a start. Josie's standing over me.

'Mommy! We're late for school.'

I struggle back to consciousness. My heart's racing, the part of me that's been on high-alert for bad news even in my sleep.

'Sorry, baby. I must not have set the alarm properly.'

We hustle to get ready; I slap together a peanut butter sandwich and grab a banana for Josie to eat in the car.

After drop-off I swing by the hospital again. Dad's hand in mine is heavy and deft and strong; his piano-player hands.

'Hi, Dad.'

The machine breathes for him, that horrible, hissing exhale. Why isn't his heart pushing back like it's supposed to? I squeeze his hand. I think of him and Josie in the kitchen; the way he listens to her re-enact the dialogue from *Moana* and *Harry Potter* like it's fresh every time.

'Come on, Dad,' I say. 'Fight harder. I know you can.'

I know you can.

*

I feel better at Bud and Branch. In the rest of my life it feels like there are too many eyes on me: Josie's worried eyes; Max's eyes, checking me over like I'm made of glass and about to break. The flowers don't watch me. They just breathe, and I breathe them in.

Molly trails around the store tweaking this and that, confiding in me about her dating life. Molly seems to have a new girlfriend every month and neither Babette nor I can keep up with the roster. Some days I could do with more quiet, but today I'm grateful for her bright voice.

I guess I'm only half paying attention to my work, though: I have to unmake a whole bouquet of what was supposed to be red roses when I accidentally do the white instead. Molly shakes her head at me, amused.

'*I'm* supposed to be the ditzy one, remember?'

Then the bell rings and I feel a pause in the air, a stiltedness. I sense Molly's eyes on me, and I look up and see Alane Brannagh standing a couple of feet inside the door.

'Dinah,' she says, with a forced brightness. Her eyes go from my face straight to my left hand, as if checking to make sure it's really true about the engagement. I see her swallow and her hand, decked out with its own giant ring of course, literally goes to her throat. She covers it though, giving the neck of her twinset a little brush-down.

I know I'm not what she had in mind for a

daughter-in-law. It was probably as big a shock to her as it was to me when Max proposed, and not a good shock in her case. She stands in the middle of the store, hands folded over her midsection, like the Queen of England making a royal visit to some slightly dirty factory.

'Alane.' I hope I sound a smidge more natural than she does. 'How are you? What can I do for you?'

'My dear.' She clears her throat. 'I'm not actually here for the flowers.' She looks around, and I almost feel she's going to start inspecting for dust.

'I was just passing by,' she goes on. 'I thought I'd stop in.'

'Oh.' I try to smile, wondering what's coming.

She takes a breath.

'We did want to mark the occasion. Seb and I wondered if you were free tonight for a' —she clears her throat—'celebratory drink.' She really has to cough out the word *celebratory*. 'Max already told us he's free tonight. He suggested I stop in here and ask you myself.'

I bite my lip. Well-intentioned, but a warning would have been good.

'Tonight?' I say.

'Unless you have plans.' She smiles her brittle smile.

Single-parenting an almost seven-year-old probably doesn't count if you're Alane Brannagh. But I know the others will happily take care of Josie for the evening. Max's family means the world to him, even if I have my doubts about them. If they're extending the olive branch, I should take it. It's just hard to pretend that this is anything like a 'normal' engagement, with the shadow of Dad hanging over everything.

'That's a nice idea, thank you,' I say.

'Shall we say six, then?'

'Six,' I confirm. 'Looking forward to it.'

Alane flashes a sort of smile at me—a baring of white veneers—and clicks towards the door.

The bell chimes as she exits and Molly looks at me.

'Lucky you,' she grins.

Lucky me, indeed.

*

'You look nice.' Max smiles as I get in the car.

I think I must look tired as hell, but I did make the effort to put on a good dress and do my hair. I figure Alane Brannagh is the kind of person who probably has shoe-trees for every pair of shoes she owns, and I don't want her looking down on me any more than she already does. I tell myself I don't need to prove anything to Alane Brannagh and I certainly don't need to *impress* her—but I just want to hold my own.

I squeeze Max's arm.

'You look nice too.'

Max, on the other hand, *does* strive to impress his family, particularly his dad. I've got glimpses from stories he's told of how it must have been for him as a teenager, trying to get approval from a father that never seemed that interested. Max would never admit that; he's too invested in the idea of having a perfect family, of being a "lucky" guy. But it's easy to see where those little things that annoy me sometimes—needing to prove he's right; taking himself a little too seriously—come from.

'I should have checked if you wanted to bring Josie,' Max says when we're on the road. 'I'm sure Mom and Dad would have been glad to see her too.'

While that's nice of him to say, I can't see Josie fitting in all that well in Alane Brannagh's everything-I-own-is-made-of-china living room.

'She and Vaughan are hanging out,' I say.

He asks me about Dad then, and I say thanks but I don't want to talk about it. I'm exhausted from thinking about it, the same cycle of dark thoughts chasing each other around my head.

Max looks a little relieved that I don't want to get into it. I suspect the truth is that he and I are on totally different wavelengths right now. If I were ready to, he'd be talking about the wedding non-stop, wanting to pin down all the details, but my heart is too consumed with everything that's going on to focus. It's too much to ask me to feel that wild rush of joy right now. Not that Max is asking me to— it's just pressure I'm putting on myself.

I know Max feels like he missed out, all those years he was working so hard on the family business, scrabbling to keep *Brannagh's* out of bankruptcy. He ate, breathed and slept the restaurant business while his friends moved away, got married, traveled, had kids. He's told me how he barely dated, didn't really have the time. His friendships suffered too—partly, I'm betting, because he was too proud to tell his friends exactly how much strain he was under and how hard he was finding it to cope. And now suddenly he's mid-thirties, eyeballing forty and thinking about the years he's missed. I know a lot of men are scared off by women with kids—they don't want to raise a child that's not theirs, and fine, whatever, I made my peace with it long ago. I'd pick Josie a million times over any man. But Max isn't like that. I think he *likes* the idea of a ready-made family. And who wouldn't love Josie?

The streets change slowly as we near his parents' house. Everything gets lusher, fancier.

'Dinah,' Max hooks a right, and glances at me. 'What do you think about a winter wedding?'

I swivel in the passenger seat.

'*This* winter?' I say. That's six months away.

'Well, but why wait?' he says.

I frown. 'It's just… what's the rush?'

'The rush?' he repeats slowly. 'I don't know, neither of us are getting any younger.' He stops. 'I figure we don't want to start trying for a kid till after the wedding, but if we get married in say, December, we could maybe have a baby by next year already.'

An unladylike sound comes out of me.

'Easy there, cowboy.'

Max's face shows no amusement.

'Look, I know we haven't fully talked through all

124

of that, but—'

'Can we pull over?' I say.

He frowns. 'Why?'

'Max, please just pull over.'

He does, frowning harder. He doesn't cut the engine though. It hums as I turn in my seat to look at him.

'Max, you're right. We *haven't* fully talked through this.' Was it stupid of me? Was I being oblivious?

'I mean,' I say slowly, 'I knew you wanted a family, but… I didn't necessarily think you wanted a baby.'

'For goodness sake, Dinah, what are you talking about?' He thrusts himself around to face me, getting tangled in his seat belt. 'That doesn't even make sense. How could I want a family and not want a baby?'

I stare at him. Family can look so many different ways—at least to me. I guess not to Max.

'*Josie*,' I say. I actually have to remind him about her—about my daughter.

Understanding spreads over his face. He doesn't look happy about it.

'Look, Dinah, Josie's a great kid. A *great* kid. But—' He looks at me. 'Really, Dinah? You didn't even think about having kids with me?'

I flush, sit back in my seat. Of course I thought about it. I just—

'I just didn't realize it was such a big deal,' I say quietly. 'I thought it would be… a *possibility*. Not a requirement.'

His face is all closed up as he turns away from me. I feel stupid now. I should have seen this coming. What he wants is fair and normal. But I can't help feeling defensive all the same. As if Josie, my perfect daughter, isn't already the most beautiful gift.

I remind myself that tons of men would be scared off by a single mom, by raising a kid that's not their own. And well, it's nice, isn't it? That Max wants to do this incredibly hard, beautiful thing with me?

I remember how it felt when Jeff and I went to the hospital for our first ultrasound: how we were tingling with excitement, knowing we were on the precipice of something huge, and how grateful I was, how perfectly I loved Jeff in that moment. But somehow it's hard to imagine doing all that again, all these years later. I'm a different person now. Now when I imagine having a brand new baby I don't think first of the tiny fingers, the pumping legs, the way you disappear down the rabbit hole of those big, world-hungry eyes. What I think of is exhaustion: bone-deep exhaustion, arguments and recriminations; calling in for take-out that takes hours to finally arrive cold and limp, because no one can even think of making dinner. I've been through all that and Max hasn't. Will he understand how much work it is? How easy it is to fight over? Will he want the hard parts, as well as the happy parts?

But more than any of that there's something else on my mind.

'Josie,' I say. 'I'd have to talk to her about it.' I

glance at him. 'She's been an only child for so long. And she's sensitive. It could be pretty destabilizing for her.'

Max stares at me.

'Wait. You want to get a seven-year-old's *permission* for you to have another kid?'

I glare back at him.

'She's not *a* seven-year-old, Max, she's *my* seven-year-old.'

Which isn't really what I mean to say. Of course it's not a question of 'permission.' But the defensive, angry feeling in my brain tells me that Max might be a *little* bit right. Planning everything around Josie isn't fair to her either—it's too much pressure. I just hate the sense that Josie's being written out of the picture in some way—in any way.

Max checks his watch.

'I guess we'll talk about this later,' he says, and indicates to pull out.

We drive on in silence.

I feel angry and guilty at the same time. Guilty towards Max, guilty towards Josie. Maybe even towards myself.

A minute later, we pull up in front of the huge, immaculate lawn, the mock-Tudor house with Alane's gunmetal green sedan parked out front. Max's parents' house is out in what I privately call Country Club Land. A big American flag waves on the flagpole. When we push open the garden gate it glides silently, not even a hint of a squeak. *Alane probably comes out to oil it every morning*, I think.

'What?' Max looks at me. Maybe I was smirking a little.

'What? Nothing,' I say.

He knocks, and we wait a minute until we hear footsteps and Alane swings the door wide.

'Darling,' she says, as Max leans in to kiss her cheek.

'Well, well, well—there they are.' We follow her into the living room, where Max's dad doesn't get out of his armchair to greet us. I'll give him the benefit of the doubt and say it's his aging knees, but most likely it's just Seb being his usual self.

'Well! Welcome to the family, Dinah,' Seb says. It sounds stilted but at least it's an effort. I thank him in a voice that's hopefully less awkward than I feel.

'Well, well, well,' he says, glancing toward the empty corners of the room as if performing for an audience. I see his eyes flick to Alane. I don't mind all that much that Max's parents don't love me, but it surprises me that Max doesn't seem to notice. But what do I know, maybe they're like this with most people.

Max seems to have rallied since our moment in the car. He's smiling now, looking from me to his parents.

'It's great, isn't it?' he says. He holds my left hand out to Alane to inspect and for a moment I have the weird feeling that the ring isn't actually mine—that even my hand isn't my own property now.

Alane gets a good, close look and then turns her gaze back to me, producing a bright smile that doesn't quite reach her eyes.

'Lovely,' she says, and I feel sure that in her mind "lovely" might apply to the ring but maybe not its bearer.

'Sit, sit,' Seb says, and we do. Max sends a little smile my way and I can see the pink flush on his cheeks. Although I wish I didn't feel quite so alone in my awkwardness, it's nice to see him happy. Despite what I think of his parents it's one of the things I like about Max—his loyalty, his commitment to family.

'My dear, are you—are you sure you're ready for this right now?' Alane says, fixing her eyes on me. 'I mean of course it's—we're very pleased, aren't we, Seb?—but what a time for you. Everything with your father. Are you *sure* this is the best moment-?'

'It's what we all need, Mom,' Max interjects. 'A happy event to look forward to. Right, Di?' He looks at me, blazing with easy conviction. My smile falters.

'I… We're all just moving forward as best we can,' I say. 'Life has to go on, right?'

Alane nods with her lips closed. There's a moment's silence.

'Drinks!' she says. 'We need drinks.'

She gets to her feet and Max does the same. I watch him follow her out into the kitchen, and I turn back to his dad. Around us the room glows in the afternoon light, its wood paneling and bay window and Hamptons-style furniture shimmering on the glossy hardwood.

'Well,' Seb clears his throat. 'And how *is* your father doing? We were so sorry to hear what happened.'

I swallow.

'Not that well, to be honest.'

How could I begin to explain to this man what it feels like going through those glass doors every day, waiting for the good news that doesn't come? And knowing I'd take every moment of this terrible limbo forever if it meant Dad not getting any worse.

'Here we are,' Alane says brightly, reappearing in the doorway with a bottle of champagne, and Max carrying a tray with four gleaming glasses.

'Seb will do the honors, won't you, dear?'

He takes the bottle and starts picking the foil cap off, and Alane takes a seat again.

'So! Have you set a date yet? For the, um, the…'

Wedding, I think. *The word you're choking over is wedding.*

Max looks at me as the champagne pops.

'Dinah's not sure about that part,' he says.

I can feel the whisper of that tense discussion in the car rearing its head again. I think Alane must catch it too. She blinks, looking between us.

'Well. Best not to rush these things, isn't it.'

The champagne fizzes as Seb pours the glasses.

Alane's face is tight as she raises her glass. I curl my fingers around the cold stem. Max and his dad raise theirs too.

'Health,' Max looks at me. 'And happiness.'

I think of Dad. Inside the glass, the bubbles fly upwards like they're trying to escape.

Escape. That sounds nice.

I take the glass to my lips, and drink.

*

Max kills the engine on the road outside our house. Through the branches of Mom's magnolia I can make out the glow of the kitchen window, all lit up and warm. For a moment I feel like a ghost in my own life—like if I floated up to that window right now, I'd see seven-year-old Dinah doing homework at the kitchen table, Dad gently guiding her through multiplication questions.

I kiss Max goodnight. I wish I could say *I had a great evening*. The car felt heavier driving home, the weight of our earlier disagreement still in the air. *Soon*, I think. *We'll talk about it soon.*

'I'll see you tomorrow,' I say.

He nods, and the car reverses and turns into the summer night.

I glance at my phone as I walk up the driveway. A missed call from Vaughan. I shouldn't have put my phone on silent. My heart quickens and I stride faster.

'Vaughan?'

I push open the front door.

I see them through the kitchen doorway: Mara at the head of the table and my sisters on each side, their heads turned towards me. My stomach flips as I see Lottie's red eyes, and the dread in all their faces as their glances meet mine.

'Dinah—it's Dad.'

Chapter Twelve
Lottie

I see Dinah's eyes widen like someone's punched her. I know what she's feeling, because when we got the news twenty minutes ago, I felt exactly the same.

'They're saying there's some issue with his lungs,' Vaughan goes on.

Dinah stares from one of us to the other.

'His lungs?' She sounds lost, disbelieving. 'But it's his heart,' she stammers. 'Nothing's wrong with his lungs.'

I swallow. That was my reaction. Even now my brain still feels like it's short-circuiting.

Mom clears her throat.

'They said it's not uncommon for patients on a pump like George,' she tells Dinah, repeating what the doctors said. 'Because his heart hasn't been pumping strongly enough, his lung function is decreasing.'

Dinah slumps into a chair.

'They said the condition's called Acute Respiratory Distress Syndrome,' Mom continues. She's clinging to the terminology as though it were a life raft; as though naming it might give us power. *If only.*

Dinah gulps the air.

'So it's... *bad*?' she says.

'He can't get enough oxygen in,' Mom goes on in her horribly calm voice. 'It could be very bad. They say it depends.'

'*It depends*,' Dinah repeats bitterly.

Everything depends. We're like puppets being jerked this way and that. No one has real answers for us.

'He's not on a ventilator yet,' Mom says. 'But they said we should anticipate it. They said it's likely to get worse during the night.'

Vaughan shakes her head. 'They didn't even act *surprised*. I don't get it. Were they *expecting* this to happen? Why didn't they warn us?'

But they have been warning us, I think. Every somber look a nurse or doctor gave us; every pause before they spoke. They've been warning us. We just didn't want to hear it.

We'd hoped so much that we were going to turn a corner... just not *this* corner, never this corner. We're not on the home stretch at all. We're doing another, terrifying lap, and everything's just getting worse.

'Does Josie know?' Dinah asks finally.

'No. We didn't know if we should tell her.'

Dinah's face already looks heavier with grief.

'Don't,' she says finally. 'There's no point. Not unless we... unless we know.'

Saying goodbye, she means. I close my eyes and pray it doesn't come to that.

'Her birthday,' I say aloud, remembering. 'Tomorrow.'

Mom draws a breath.

'Let her have her party,' she says, and I hear all that she's not saying beneath the words.

Let her be happy a little longer.

Let there be one more night of laughter.

*

I can't sleep again tonight.

Not that I expected to.

I pick up my phone and wake the screen. The time illuminates: 1:40. I hesitate.

Are you awake? I text Roman.

Roman's been an unexpected support these last few days. Our months together have been fun, but not exactly deep—which is why I wouldn't have expected him to be so present, and so kind, as he's been since Dad's collapse.

I'm awake, he texts.

I stare at the phone screen for a while.

Can I come over?

The three dots appear, then disappear. I feel stupid. It's too late to invite myself over.

Of course, finally appears on my screen.

I pull on some clothes, move quietly down the stairs, and start the car. I can't bear another sleepless night staring up at my ceiling, and I'll only be a phone call away.

Roman buzzes me in and is waiting for me upstairs. The sight of him belongs to another world, one where everything is still normal. The electric light bounces off his bronze skin, and his hair is all fluffy dark coils, not gelled the way it usually is when he meets me. His face is open and waiting.

'Hi.'

I don't know what to say. Small talk doesn't exist anymore.

'Come in.' He spreads the door wide, and I step into the tiny kitchen.

'Do you want to sit up for a bit?'

Even though it's late his eyes are focused, full of concern. He seems older than he really is. I remember when I first started going to the bar where he worked. He'd felt free to tease me, even though we'd barely met.

'Is this your thing, the teen-movie sexy librarian vibe?' He'd nodded to my fitted grey tunic, my square-rim glasses and ponytail. 'You're going to take off those glasses and shake out your mane in a minute?'

I'd flushed.

'This is just how I dress.'

He'd shrugged and smiled, not embarrassed to have embarrassed me. Not rushing to make up for any offense he might have caused. Just smiling and pushing a fresh cocktail my way, and trusting that I knew he meant no harm.

Now he boils water and plucks some mint from a pot on his windowsill. He pours the brew and pushes a cup in front of me.

'Tell me.'

I close my eyes and talk. I tell him about today's

turn for the worse. What we know and don't know. I tell him about the nightmares and the sleeplessness, and this feeling I have when I see Dad, as if death is in the room too and trying to steal him.

Roman nods cautiously, though I can tell he doesn't follow all of it.

'And...' I bite my lip. 'I know this sounds selfish, but on top of everything... my future.'

'Have you told the Culinary Institute?' Roman says. 'I'm sure they'd defer your place, or—'

I shake my head. I'm not naive. You don't have a cardiac arrest and just "bounce back". Whatever happens, Mom is going to need help. She's going to need me.

That window is closed.

'You don't know,' Roman says. 'Things might look different in—'

'Please just stop, Roman. I'm not going.'

Roman frowns, but he drops it.

I start to tell him about Bonnie, then. About what the nurse said. About the old boxes of hers upstairs I've been going through, and how *real* they made her seem.

'Why would he say her name?' I shake my head. 'Why *her*?'

Roman shrugs, and collects our mugs. He gives me one of his old T-shirts to sleep in. I climb into bed and reach for him, sliding my hand under his shirt to the warm skin.

'Lottie?' He catches my hand as I try to tug off his

shirt. 'Are you sure? I mean, with what you've been going through and—'

'Shh,' I say. 'I'm sure.'

I tug the shirt over his head. Because more than anything right now, what I need is to forget. A moment of oblivion, a moment of escape.

He relaxes, smiling down at me. And then together, we help me forget.

*

I wake thirsty, headachy. I find a painkiller in Roman's bathroom cabinet and go to the sink, run a glass of water. There's a drunk on the street outside, thumping into the recycling bins and singing scraps of some old song. Glass clinks and jangles into the gutter. It's almost dawn.

Don't you dare take him, Bonnie, I think, and the viciousness of the feeling surprises me. *Don't you dare take him away from us.*

I go back to bed and toss and turn some more.

At work, Vaughan rings me to say they've put Dad on the ventilator.

I sleepwalk through the work day, then stop in at the bookstore on Elm Street on my way home. I want Josie to get what joy she can get out of the day, but I admit I wish this little birthday party had been canceled.

I pluck the Lemony Snicket box set from the shelves and the lady at the desk wraps it for me, smiling.

'Birthday?' she says, and I nod.

'My niece,' I manage.

'I hope she has a wonderful day!' She beams. I don't trust myself to speak.

Back at home Dinah's in the living room, arranging a birthday banner. Her eyes are red-rimmed but there's a stubborn determination in them too. Dinah's the one who never gives up.

I envy her that strength.

'Where's Josie?' I say.

'Trisha's bringing her with Ashanti.'

She looks my way when she speaks but her glance doesn't linger. I wish we were still the kind of sisters who could support each other at a time like this.

Upstairs I drop my bag, look through my wardrobe for a change of clothes. A sunbeam falls on Bonnie's doll like a spotlight, making her dark hair glow orange. I go to the bookshelf and pick her up. She really does look like Josie, just more… forbidding. Her lips purse together in that dollish way like she's disapproving of me. Her head is still tilted at an angle and today it bothers me, like I'm being mocked somehow. I try to angle it and twist the other way. The porcelain squeaks as the head comes off in my hand, and something falls out.

Downstairs the doorbell rings but I ignore it, turning over the little paper in my hand. It's thin and delicate. I can see the ink coming through as I fold it open. The note's handwritten. *Bonnie the packrat*, I think. What is it she was keeping in here?

I guess I shouldn't, but I smooth it out and begin to

read.

Dearest B, it begins.

And as I read on I sink onto the bed, my legs weak.

Impossible, I think. But it's not impossible, it's the truth. Right there in black and white. I just can't believe what it says.

George

George doesn't know where the water came from. At some point it just began. It's an ocean now, all around him. It's tiring. Maybe if he just stopped, and let the water carry him. It wants to take him somewhere, doesn't it?

That's when he sees her again: the wispy figure in the dark. She shines out of it like a beacon. She's waiting for him, isn't she? That's where the water is taking him.

It's you, George says, or tries to say. Because he knows her now. She's the one who betrayed him, isn't she?

He tries to put his feet down in the current, but he splutters and goes under. When he looks up again the figure is still there, watching, her face impassive. And doubt comes over George.

Was it she who betrayed him? Or was he the one who betrayed her? George shakes his head, kicks against the current.

But his kick is small and feeble. A wave crashes over him and then there's only stillness, the silence of the universe ringing in his ears.

Chapter Thirteen
Dinah

I close the front door behind Trisha as Josie and Ashanti disappear into the living room in a flurry of excitement. Trisha pulls a bottle of wine from a brightly-colored bag.

'There's a birthday gift in here too, but this one's for the grown-ups.'

I smile weakly and we go into the kitchen.

'How're you holding up, honey?' she says. I texted her earlier about Dad and the respiratory issue.

'Well, you know.' I shrug. I don't know how to begin to answer.

She gives my arm a quick squeeze. 'I'm praying for you.'

My throat constricts. It's a gift being able to express sympathy like Trisha does—it's so matter-of-fact you don't feel pitied, but so real you can't doubt it. I fish two wine glasses from the cupboard and set them on the table.

'Better make it three. Rayna texted she was on her way.'

Rayna is Lewis's mom.

'Josie's father's back in town.' I fill Trisha in as I take a third glass from the cabinet. 'He'll be stopping by too.'

Trisha raises an eyebrow.

'Jeff, right?'

I nod.

'I thought he wasn't in your lives these days.'

'He wasn't. Hopefully he doesn't mess things up this time and I don't have to kill him.'

Trisha's mouth quirks up at the corners.

'Now there's the Dinah I know.'

Vaughan pokes her head around the kitchen door.

'Hi, Trisha,' she says, and I see how tired her smile is. I bet she didn't sleep last night either.

'Grandma, come help us with the balloons!' I hear Josie say across the hall. We all move into the living room just as Lewis and Rayna show up. The girls squeal and manhandle Lewis into their balloon-blowing corner. I hear Ashanti taking charge, telling the other two which color balloons go with which. Trisha rolls her eyes and grins.

'I'm raising a dictator,' she says.

'To strong women,' Rayna says and lifts her glass. She pats my back; she knows about Dad too.

'Strong women,' I echo quietly.

I hear Lottie's feet on the stairs—she's taken her time joining us. Then out the window I see Jeff coming up the path. He's in a fresh shirt, gel in his hair, carrying a bouquet of flowers. Josie must have spotted him too because she barrels out of the living room, eyes bright.

I open the door and Jeff grins, and hands over

the flowers. 'These are for you, birthday girl.'

'No one's ever bought me flowers!' She beams at him. I feel a little embarrassed at that. I *work* in a florist's. I guess there's something about the things we take for granted.

'Here, sweetie. Let me put them in water,' I say. I can see it's hard for her to let me take them but she does.

Jeff follows me to the kitchen door, just out of Josie's earshot.

'Di, quick question,' he murmurs. 'What are your feelings about piñatas?'

I look at him. 'You brought a *piñata*?'

'Well, the other day, she said she wanted one…' He trails off, looking doubtful.

I shake my head. 'Okay, sure. Get the piñata.'

The kids go ape when they see it—a neon-colored unicorn about the same size as Josie. Any other year I'd worry about Mara's reaction to us getting paper unicorn innards all over her carpet, but we're beyond that now. My phone beeps: Max, texting to apologize that he's running late.

Soon the living room is filled with the remains of two extra-large pizzas, and the babble of three sugar-high seven-year-olds competing over who gets to attack the piñata first. I push the pain from my chest and focus. Vaughan hands Josie the bat and my daughter grins, bouncing on the spot. I try to hook the bandana over her eyes.

'Stay still, Jojo.' Vaughan shakes her head. 'She

can't get the blindfold on with you jitterbugging like that.'

I spin her around three times and let her go.

Ashanti goes next, and then Lewis, none of them getting any strikes in. When Lewis's blindfold comes off, Josie fixes on me.

'Mommy!' She thrusts out her finger. 'You're next!'

I shake my head. 'That piñata's not for grown-ups.'

'I don't know about that,' Trisha says, giving me a nudge.

'What?' She shrugs when I look at her. 'Could be cathartic.'

'Mommy's turn!' Josie calls.

Jeff appears to take my drink from my hand. 'I'll hold that.'

I admit defeat, and let Vaughan fit the bandana around my eyes and spin me. Maybe I've drunk more of Trisha's wine than I realized, because the spinning definitely makes me dizzy. How can one little bandana make everything so dark?

Vaughan puts the bat in my hands and I swing, and hear the gust of an indrawn breath beside me. It's Lottie, I can tell. I know that sound she makes, that girlish little gasp. It's something about the darkness, maybe, and the wine, but suddenly I'm back to that night in the attic, years ago. Me standing at the window, looking down onto the dark night. What I saw then, and how nothing's been the same since.

I swing the bat again and there's a gale of laughter

from the kids.

'Missed it!' Ashanti jeers happily. Just for her benefit I brandish the stick and hear them cackling.

'The other way, Mommy!' Josie says loyally before someone shushes her.

Then the darkness seems to deepen. I feel exposed, suddenly—as if everyone in the room is looking at me and seeing not just a silly blindfolded woman, but everything else that I'm struggling to keep hidden. My fears laid out for public consumption: fears that Dad will get worse, that he'll never make it home to us; fears about Max, that he wants things I won't be able to give. Fears about Josie. That I'll disappoint her. That she'll get older and resent me and the choices I've made. Suddenly inside the blindfold it's impossibly dark.

'Swing, Mommy!' Josie's sweet voice calls, but I can't. I try to move, I *want* to move, but it's like the world's closing in on me and I can't move a muscle.

And then I feel a hand on my shoulder, guiding me. The scent of him is still the same after all these years, reminding me of when we used to dance together. And I guess it's a little like dancing now—an awkward, clumsy first dance—as Jeff steers me where I need to go. Pivot, turn, step, step. I force my body to trust him, I tell it that trusting just this much, just this once, won't hurt us.

The room is quiet now, but it feels like a different kind of quiet.

'No cheating!' Vaughan's voice says, joking on the

surface but with something underneath it.

'High and to the right,' Jeff murmurs, and then his hand releases.

I raise the bat high and swing.

Smash. The impact travels up my arm and there's the skittery sound of candies falling. I tug off the bandana, feeling my shoulders sag with relief. Josie's friends are shrieking, scooping candies from the floor, their hair already coated in glitter. Trisha's laughing, even Vaughan and Mara are sort of smiling. No one's looking at me except for Josie. She's not scuttling around on the floor with her friends. She's just standing there, watching me, then watching Jeff.

I shake my head at her. 'They'll get all your candy, Jojo! Get in there. Use your elbows!'

Trisha laughs at me.

'You're incorrigible,' she says. 'Don't corrupt her.'

I force a smile and excuse myself to the kitchen. It's not the nearness to Jeff that has unsettled me, at least not in a romantic way. It's just the weight of memories, the gut-punch of realizing just how much time has passed and how different things are from how they used to be. And Josie's delight in having Jeff around. It's so natural, but I wish it didn't mean so much to her.

'Hey, Di?'

I turn around. Jeff's followed me in.

'I just want to say thanks for letting me be here with you all today.'

'You're welcome here, Jeff.' I meet his eyes. There's a lot we're not saying. The ways he let us down. The ways I made him leave. The way all I've ever wanted to do is protect my daughter from pain.

'Just don't hurt her,' I say before I can stop myself. I don't mean to, it just slips out. Jeff just looks at me.

'I won't,' he says quietly.

I go to the fridge and ease out the cake. Then I turn to count the dishes from the cabinet, keeping busy until I hear Jeff quietly leave the room. I exhale. Today is too much.

The doorbell pulls me back. Max.

I swing the door open with a rush of relief that surprises me. I think it surprises him too.

'Everything okay, babe?'

I nod, trying not to tear up.

'Sorry I'm late,' he says. He has an elaborately wrapped present under one arm. He kisses me and steps inside.

'Josie.' I stop her as she scoots by, socks skating fast on the floors. 'Come say hi. Max brought you something.'

She stops, looks up at Max.

'Thank you.'

'You can open it now if you like,' I say. She glances back to the living room, where the others are, and I can feel her pull towards them. She turns back and looks down at the box in her hands, carefully picks one flap free and then the other. It's a Barbie. A soccer-playing Barbie.

The soccer part is cute, I guess—Josie plays soccer, Max knows that. But I've always been pleased that Josie's never shown an interest in Barbies.

She looks at it dubiously, then at me. She probably knows my feelings about Barbies too, but a gift is a gift. You make exceptions. I try to show her my encouraging face so she won't wrinkle up her nose like she's kind of doing now.

'Oh man.' Jeff's passing through the hall. 'A Barbie! That's old school.'

I don't think he means it badly but it weighs down our awkward moment even more and I sense Max bristle.

'I'm sure you brought something nice, Jeff,' he says.

I can feel the edge there and no doubt Jeff feels it too. I think even Josie feels it. It seems to remind us all how little Jeff has to show for himself as a father.

'Daddy brought me flowers,' Josie says. 'And a piñata.' It pains me to hear the defensiveness in her voice; she probably doesn't even know exactly what she's defending Jeff against.

'Oh,' Max says. 'Flowers. That's nice.'

He's not sneering, but his voice is cool. There's a pause, and then Jeff's face dissolves into a smile, a smile I've seen a million times before. It's his I'm-not-gonna-fight smile, the one he gives right before making a quick exit.

'Well,' he says, all breezy suddenly. 'Thanks so

much for letting me stop by, Di. This was really nice. Josie, birthday girl, I'll see you soon, okay? Max.' He tips his head. And within moments he's walking down the driveway.

I suppress a sigh—I feel irritated at him, and at Max. I look at Josie's face and it's stormy, a tiny bit mutinous. And Josie is not a mutinous child.

'Cake!' Vaughan calls from the living room, and my daughter goes silently back inside. Max looks at me, and I look back at him.

As we sing the birthday song I can't help remember Jeff singing it to Josie years ago, when she was just a little thing. I hope she doesn't have those memories too. Memories are a trap, sometimes. They're too hard to let go of.

I wait until everyone who wants one has got a second slice, and then I start to clear the plates. Trisha whispers to the kids and starts to gather their things.

She presses my hand on the way out.

'Oh, Dinah,' she says. 'You take care. All of you.'

I squeeze back.

'Hang in there,' Rayna says.

They drive away.

Vaughan and Mara and Max are in the kitchen; Lottie's disappeared again. The living room feels desolate, the battered unicorn grotesque.

I put my head around the kitchen door.

'Where's Josie?'

Mara looks at me.

'She went to get ready for bed. She seemed a little... tired.'

Josie *never* puts herself to bed—going to sleep while the rest of us are still awake is pretty much her least favorite thing. Max gives me a significant look. I'm guessing "tired" is a euphemism here. And I'm pretty sure I know why she's upset. My heart sinks.

I go quietly up the stairs and tap on our door.

'Jojo?'

There's silence.

I nudge the door open and she's in her pajamas, already in bed.

'Baby bear,' I say. 'What's going on?'

She gives me a look.

'Why did Max make Daddy leave?'

I bite my tongue. Yes, I'm annoyed at Max for not handling all this more graciously, but Jeff and his crab-scuttle out of here played its own part. More than annoyance, it just makes my heart sink: if this is what happens when Jeff leaves a party, what's it going to be like when he leaves town altogether? I feel a wave of anger at him all over again: for being so charming, for being so damn *likable* and yet lacking the ability to follow through. He makes people love him, and then doesn't take responsibility for the feelings he creates.

I should know.

I sigh and sit down on the opposite bed.

'You know, Jo-bear... we may be adults, but none of us are perfect,' I say. 'Not Max, not your Daddy, and not me. But we do all want you to be happy.'

She huffs a little, but the corners of her mouth turn down less than before.

'Max probably didn't say the right thing,' I add. 'But he also didn't *make* anyone leave. Different people react differently when they're feeling uncomfortable.'

'But why are they uncomfortable?' She frowns.

Because they're men, I think wryly.

'Because life,' I say to Josie, and she rolls her eyes at me. Wow—I wonder if she's been waiting to turn seven to pull that on me.

'I hate it when you say that.'

'I know,' I say, and kiss her forehead. 'I love you so much, Josie-bear.'

She huffs again. I kiss her two more times and she makes a little exasperated noise.

'*Okay,*' she concedes. 'I love you too.'

'I know,' I say again. 'But thank you for telling me.' And I plant one more smacker of a kiss on her for good measure.

When I get back downstairs Max raises an eyebrow.

I sink down onto the couch beside him and he hands me my wine glass. I look at him.

'That was hard.'

'I hope you weren't too tough on her. It wasn't really her fault.'

I frown. Of course 'it' wasn't her fault.

'I don't mean I was *reprimanding* her, Max. I meant

I had to *talk* to her. She was unhappy.'

He stiffens.

'She was sulking, you mean.'

'No, *sulking* is not what I mean.' I feel a wave of anger and I have to remind myself that he meant it innocently. He's not a parent, after all. 'Josie's not a sulky child, she's a sensitive one. There's a difference, Max.'

His face tightens.

'You know,' I say. 'Josie is an incredibly well-behaved kid. If you don't think *she*'s well-behaved, you're in for a rude awakening if you ever become a dad.'

'Thanks for the *if*, Dinah,' he says coolly. 'You've made your feelings clear on that.'

I feel a pang—partly guilt, partly anger.

'Max, don't be like this—come on.'

I just want him to *understand.* I don't mean to hurt him. I just want him to stop making assumptions about what I want, then blaming me for feeling differently.

He looks at me.

'Dinah... how do you think I feel? I ask you to marry me, you say you need time, and then just when I think we're on track suddenly your ex is back in town and he's all over everything.'

I shake my head.

'Max, it's not like that. I don't want Jeff. I want you.'

He looks down at the car keys clenched in his

hand.

'I sure hope so, Dinah,' he says, then leaves the room.

*

It's the middle of the night when I startle awake. I was dreaming of Dad again. I lie there for a while, listening to Josie's breathing. Then I pull on socks and pad downstairs. I flip the kitchen light on and there's a yelp, and I yell out too.

'Vaughan.'

My heart's still racing. 'What are you doing here in the dark?'

She just shakes her head, squinting in the sudden brightness, and now I can see she's been crying.

I kill the overhead lights and turn on a side-lamp. She sniffs and pulls at the collar of her pajamas. Others might sleep in ratty old T-shirts. Not Vaughan: perfect matching pajamas, without fail. I bet she never misses a step of her skincare routine either.

'What's wrong?' I say. She just shakes her head. Maybe it's a stupid question. Dad is what's wrong, for all of us. But this is so unlike my sister. I slide the near-empty mug from under her hands and give it a sniff. I heat the water again and slice a fresh lemon, then tip in another dash of bourbon. I find a second mug and do the same for myself.

'Here.' I slide it back over the table to her.

'Thank you,' she says, the first time she's opened her mouth. She doesn't sound like herself. She sounds like someone much younger than my super-competent big sister.

'It's stupid.' She shakes her head.

'What's stupid?' I say.

'It's stupid that Mitchell and I are fighting about this *now*, when everything's so crazy. I feel bad that I'm even *thinking* about anything else, honestly…'

So this is about Mitchell.

'You and Mitchell fight?' I don't know why that surprises me exactly. Mitchell is the kind of guy that always seems a bit too pleased with himself for my taste, but I guess it's understandable. He's about as annoyingly perfect in his way as Vaughan is in hers. Gregarious, ambitious, smart.

Vaughan says nothing.

'You can tell me.' I make the cross-my-heart sign we'd always do as kids, waiting for Vaughan to shake her head at the throwback. But she just looks at me with a quiet, sad face, and I realize how long ago it was since we were two little girls telling our secrets in this house. Suddenly I see us from a birds-eye view, the way I've always imagined Mom seeing us. And I see how grown-up we truly are, how far our problems are from the little-girl problems they used to be. And I wish they weren't.

I really wish they weren't.

'It's… complicated,' Vaughan says.

I raise my eyebrows at her.

'Mitchell…' She stops. 'Mitchell really doesn't want kids.'

'And wait, you *do*? I thought—'

'I know, I know. I didn't always,' she snaps. Vaughan loves kids and she adores Josie. But not every woman who loves kids wants one of her own—which is a point I've heard Vaughan make numerous times over the years.

'I was never exactly *against* having kids,' she points out. 'I just thought… well, life's good, why change it? But then… I don't know, I just started to think differently. And please'—her voice rises—'don't give me some cliché about the "biological clock." I'm more than just some, some *mammal.*'

'I wasn't going to,' I murmur. I've rarely seen Vaughan like this.

'I just started to feel like…' She gestures, and a little liquid sloshes from her mug. 'I mean, Mitchell is good, our marriage is good—well, you know. We work at it; it's fine. Work is fine. But I guess I realized… none of it is going to *change* that much anymore, you know? Or only change in sad ways, like… like Dad getting sick, or all of us just getting older, and… aside from the things that slow down or get worse, everything's just going to stay the same.'

That seems a little pessimistic, I want to say, but she's looking at me, searching my face for understanding.

'I mean,' she says, 'I'm grateful, I know how lucky I am, but… I have all this energy, all this… *stuff* to give… so where's it all going to go? I can't spend all of it at work. I can't spend all of it on Mitchell.' She looks at me. 'Am I being selfish? Is that a selfish

156

reason to have a kid?'

'No,' I say. 'Wanting to give your gifts to someone is a *good* thing.'

She sniffs.

'And then, after everything with Dad....' she goes on. 'I'd been talking about this to Mitchell before, but I guess he didn't really think I was serious. Maybe *I* didn't even know if I was serious. But I woke up that morning after Dad got taken to the hospital and I had this thought, *I don't want to be the end of the line*. You have Josie. I don't want to be the end of my line. I want there to be someone that comes after me. Someone for the future.'

I say nothing. I don't know what to say. It sounds like she's pretty clear on this.

'That's a real downer, huh?' She turns to me, laugh-crying.

I shake my head, then scooch my hand over the table onto hers.

'And Mitchell?' I say after a while. 'He really won't...?'

She releases my hand and sits back in her chair, shaking her head.

'He says I'm just reacting to stress right now, and that we made our decision not to have kids for good reasons, and now is not the time to throw those good reasons out the window.' She winces.

'So what are you gonna do?' I say. 'Do you think you can change his mind?'

She shrugs. 'I don't know. His own family never

got on well... I guess he doesn't have good memories of, you know, the whole "family" thing.'

'But if you and he had a family, it wouldn't be anything like how his was,' I say.

Vaughan looks at me. '*I* know that. And maybe rationally *he* knows that. But these things aren't always rational, Di.'

I huff. 'Well, he can't expect you to just accept him being *ir*rational.'

She shrugs again. 'Well, what then—an ultimatum? And *that's* how we bring a kid into this world? Because I've forced him into it?'

We're silent for a moment.

How unfair, I think; how ironic. Here's Vaughan married to a man who doesn't want the kids she's aching for, and I'm marrying one whose impatience for fatherhood scares me. I think of Josie upstairs, her little forehead furrowed in sleep, and then at the glimmering stone on my finger. *Why can't what we have be enough*, that's what I kept thinking, after I heard how Max really felt about more kids. *When we have so much.*

I wonder what Daddy would say to that. Maybe he'd tell me I've got it all wrong; maybe he'd say that you can never have too much joy—that we should stockpile every shot we have at it whenever we get the chance. After all, you never know when the good things you have will end.

'I'm sorry, Vee,' I say finally, because anything like

it'll all be fine is a useless phrase to throw around in a situation like this. It feels strange to be the comforter—it's not a role I'm used to with Vaughan, who never seems to need anything from anyone. Usually Vaughan's the one impatient with me for not pulling everything together as neatly as she does. I worry she'll think I'm being patronizing now. But she just looks at me and squeezes my hand.

'Come on,' she says. 'Let's go to bed.'

In my head, I can hear the old phrase Dad used to fall back on when we were little: *It'll all seem better in the morning.*

If only that were true.

I walk up the stairs behind Vaughan, thinking how full of secrets this family of ours is. Secrets festering like old wounds… and if we're not careful, they'll kill us from the inside out.

Chapter Fourteen
Lottie

Moonlight slices through my window and across the room. I know I'm not the only one still awake—I heard Vaughan crying quietly in her room when I got up to use the bathroom, and I heard Dinah's bedroom door open and close not long ago. I turn over, knowing I won't sleep.

The birthday party would have felt surreal in any case, but I felt like I was sleepwalking through it after I found that note.

I snap on the light and rummage under my pillow, pulling it out once more.

Darling B—
Happy birthday, my getaway girl. I can't wait to see you this weekend. I've bought you something that I know you will look fabulous in…
You know, I was always told that there was no room in this world for weakness. But you're my weakness, Bonnie, and this world was made for you.
Your
C

I stare at that last initial. It's very definitely a "C", not a "G." And it's dated, too: this isn't from before she married Dad.

Beloved, perfect Bonnie. Flawless wife and mother. *She* was cheating on Dad? I sigh and put the note back under my pillow. I can't get my head around it.

What would Dad think if he knew about all this?

What would *Dinah* think? She worships the memory of her mother.

I roll over, hearing or just imagining the rustle of the note under my pillow.

Your C.

Calvin, Charles, Chris, Carlos? It might as well be a needle in a haystack.

I feel like shouting at Bonnie that she's a hypocrite. Lying to Dad, lying to her daughters. And making Mom and me live with these myths; with the ghost of her always here, like stale air in the back of a closet.

I push the slip of paper back under my pillow and turn off the light. And don't sleep.

And don't sleep.

And don't sleep.

*

I stand on one side of the hospital cot, Mom on the other.

Please come back, Dad, I think at him, my whole brain seizing with it. I guess it's my imagination, but for a moment I could swear something passes between us. Some beat, some burst of warmth. I wait, trying to decide if it was real or not. But all I hear is the ventilator, that horrible death-rattle sound it makes.

Please, lungs. Be strong.

Be stronger.

Mom catches my eye, and I know she feels it too, the little hope-prayers I'm sending up like paper lanterns.

He hasn't got worse overnight, the doctors say, but he hasn't got any better. In the car a text from Roman chirps on my phone.

How are you?

I put the phone away. I don't even know.

'You want me to drop you at work?' Mom says, and I nod.

'Mom?'

She blinks.

'Can I ask you something?' I hesitate. 'Dad and Bonnie... were they happy?'

She takes her eyes from the road to frown at me.

'This was all so long ago, Lottie.'

'I know,' I say. 'I'm just... thinking about it.'

She sighs, then shrugs.

'Were they happy? Yes and no, I guess...'

'What do you mean?'

Mom pauses. I can hear the reluctance in her voice. 'Well, they loved each other. But... Bonnie was a very restless soul, I think. It wasn't that your dad wanted to curtail her freedom, but I think it hurt him that she wanted so much of it.' We hit a red light and she sits back in the driver's seat.

'What kind of freedom?' I say.

'Well… the job, for one thing. At Brannagh's. Your dad was all for her having a job, but not that one. The hours were so antisocial. He had to put your sisters to bed alone most nights, make them dinner by himself. Working there was just something Bonnie did because she loved the buzz, you know? It gave her a second identity, I guess. Brannagh's was kind of a flashy place back then. I think it kind of hurt your Dad's feelings, to be honest.'

I turn that over. I wonder if it was the kind of "flashy place" where wealthy diners chatted up their waitresses and got their phone numbers. I consider for a split second telling Mom about the note… but what good would that do now?

'He never forgave them for firing her, though,' she says as the light turns green.

'They fired her?' I say. 'From Brannagh's?'

Mom shrugs again. 'Well, Bonnie probably wasn't the most reliable employee they'd ever seen.'

'Does Dinah know that?' I ask. I just thought Dad didn't like the Brannaghs because they were stuck up.

Mom frowns. 'Maybe not. Your father can be protective, you know, about things to do with Bonnie.'

We're silent then for a moment.

'What was it like?' I say quietly. 'Falling in love with someone who… who was going through all that?'

Mom looks at me.

'It wasn't like that at first,' she says. 'I was just a friend. Not even a friend, just a friendly face who lived down the street.' She pauses. 'I felt terrible for him, but I didn't want to get involved, not at first. I saw some of the women around here, the way they were circling. Grief is like catnip to some women. But that was never what I wanted. It was just… we were friends. We had things in common. He knew he could talk to me and I would listen, and above all he knew I would be honest with him and not pull punches. Which is why I told him when it had gone on long enough—the grieving, I mean, or the worst of the grieving. I told him he needed to pull himself together for the girls' sake.' She pauses. 'And he did, you know. Overnight.'

'Was it really bad?' I say. 'Before?'

'He fell apart,' Mom says bluntly. 'He just… he looked so ill. It was like he was trying to find his way into the grave himself.'

I stare out the window, and wonder about all the things I didn't see. I guess children always want to believe their parents are strong, that they're bigger and braver than whatever the world can throw at them. And now I think, maybe parents letting them believe that isn't arrogance or wishful thinking. Maybe it's a gift. An act of grace. It's just one of our family truths that Daddy is the one everybody counts on; the one we all agree on. The lynchpin. Now I wonder whether it's sometimes been hard for Mom to go along with that system. She could never have let slip any suggestion that Daddy wasn't "perfect" in front of Dinah, or even Vaughan.

Or even me.

Suddenly I wonder if it's ever felt lonely for her.

*

The day passes in a blur. My boss reminds me that I still have "personal days" allocated through the end of this quarter, but these little illusions of normalcy—the grey-and-chrome fittings, my particleboard desk and beaten-up swivel chair—give me something to cling to, something that feels almost like "before".

Soon my cubicle-mate Brent is slinging his satchel over his shoulder and I hear him wish Vashti on his other side a good weekend before he turns back and gives me an awkward look. I guess he knows there's no good weekend ahead for some of us.

I gather my things and head for the elevator. But instead of going home I keep walking. Down Lincoln Street, down Park, across Beech, and…

Brannagh's.

There it is. The green awning flaps in the breeze. I can see through the windows that it's bustling. I push open the swing door and look around as I wait to be seated. Brannagh's is kind of an institution in Birch Bend and yet I've never been through the doors. Little wonder, since Dad never wanted to come. But talking with Mom about it got me curious. I wanted to at least take a look at the place from inside.

The hostess brings me to a spot at the bar and hands me a menu. I turn it over, looking for something that isn't a full meal. The last page has black-and-white pictures of the restaurant through the years, with staff group photos. I'm not really expecting to see Bonnie but I search them anyway.

'Hi there.' The waitress comes by almost immediately. Her grey hair is pulled up in a twist above a statement necklace. 'I'm Andrea, and I'll be taking care of you tonight. Would you like to hear about our specials?'

I ask if I can just get a salad and she nods. 'Boston Bibb or Arugula?'

'Um. Boston.'

'You got it. You want to hold onto that?' She nods at the menu.

'Yes, please.' I know she means for another order, but I'm not through looking at the old photos.

I see her checking in on other tables on her way back to the kitchen, patting customers on the shoulder or laughing with them. It looks like she has a real regular crowd here. I wonder if that's what it was like for Bonnie.

When she comes back with my salad the menu's still open in front of me to the photo page.

'Oh, gosh.' Andrea chuckles. 'You're checking out the dinosaur years.' She shakes her head. 'Let me tell you, the shoes they used to make us wear...'

I look up. 'You worked here back then?'

She nods, tapping her finger against one of the figures in a group photo.

'That's me,' she says. 'Great hair, am I right?'

I look at the photo again. Now that she says it, the resemblance is clear. I hesitate.

'My dad's first wife was a waitress here for a while. Bonnie Spencer?'

I see her pause and frown as the penny drops.

'Oh, wow. Yeah, I remember. Poor girl.'

It gives me a little chill to know that she remembers Bonnie and the accident; it's like she knows a little piece of our history.

'That was a long time ago,' she says finally.

I nod.

'I barely met your dad, honey, but he seemed like a nice man. I was sorry such a terrible thing should've happened to him. I'm glad he found somebody new.'

'Thank you,' I say awkwardly.

She refills my water glass.

'I hope you don't mind me asking,' I say slowly. 'But... I heard she was fired. I guess you don't remember anything about that?'

Andrea looks at me.

'What do you mean?'

'Well... why she was fired,' I say. I can feel my cheeks flushing.

She clears her throat. 'Your dad probably knows more about it than I would, honey. I wouldn't set much store by the gossip.'

'So there was gossip?'

Andrea looks uncomfortable.

'There was always gossip in this place.' She looks at me and sighs. 'One of the girls overheard she'd stolen something. That's all I remember.' She wipes the lip of the pitcher with a napkin and sets it back down.

Theft? I turn that over. *Would* Bonnie have stolen money—for the high of it, the way a teenager would? Or because she needed it... but what would she have needed it for?

'Did you know her well?' I say. 'Bonnie?'

Andrea glances at me. 'You sure do have a lot of questions about her.'

'Yeah.' I clear my throat. 'It's just my dad doesn't talk about her much.'

Andrea half-smiles.

'Well, she was just one of those girls. Seemed like she'd been born on thin ice. Always pushing the envelope, you know? Independent as they come.'

So that's where Dinah gets it.

'She was a popular waitress,' Andrea goes on. 'The boys loved her, you know? She always got the best tips.'

I feel a little twist when she says that.

'Was there... anyone in particular?' I say. 'I mean... anyone who didn't pay much attention to the wedding ring?'

Andrea laughs drily. 'Honey, half the men who came in here could've fit that description. I'm not sure anybody knew the difference between harassment and flirtation back then.' She pauses, remembering something. 'Did your daddy and Mikey Cahill ever make it up?'

I look at her. Mikey Cahill?

'I'm sorry… I don't know who that is.'

'Well, I guess that's a no, then.' She looks off, checking the room or remembering old times, I can't tell.

'Mikey worked with your dad. He was a pal of your mom's too, I think. He came in here almost every day for his lunch. Sweet boy. I just remember he and your dad had such a falling out after her funeral.' She sighs. 'Grief'll do that to people.'

There's a pause. I can almost feel my brain pulsing.

'What was the name again?' I ask.

'Cahill,' she says. 'Mikey Cahill.'

Cahill, I think. *C for Cahill. Why not?*

'Enjoy.' Andrea nods down at my salad. 'Nice chatting with you.'

She leaves me to eat in silence, alone with my whirring carousel of thoughts.

*

'So, I found this stuff,' I tell Roman when I get to his place. I'm still buzzing with the conversation at Brannagh's. 'Bonnie, my dad's first wife? She was having an affair.'

'Really?' He makes a face. 'Huh. Do you think your dad knew?'

'No… I don't know.' I frown. 'And then, I just

169

went to this restaurant where she used to work,' I go on. 'Brannagh's? And someone there said she was fired for *theft*. Isn't that wild?'

Roman eyes me.

I'm expecting him to chime in and agree how shocking the whole thing is, maybe to offer to look into this Mikey Cahill thing with me, but instead he just looks... disappointed?

He puts his hand on mine.

'Lottie, I don't mean this in a bad way, but... you're starting to sound kind of obsessed with this woman. I agree, the affair—if there really was an affair—is a weird thing to find out. But... you know she's not the actual reason your dad is in the hospital?'

It's strange, the feeling in my body when he says that. I know what he's saying is true. Obviously it's true. But a little part of me resents him for saying it.

Because yes, I *would* like this to be all Bonnie's fault.

'You don't get it,' I say sharply.

He doesn't know what it is to be in my shoes; what it is to owe your life to a tragedy. I wouldn't be *alive* if Bonnie hadn't died. Other people get to be grateful for their lives without knowing someone else had to die for that to happen.

'I just want it to make sense,' I say. 'I just want to know why things happened the way they did.'

Because if Bonnie's death was a random tragedy that was never supposed to happen, what does that say about me?

That I was never supposed to exist?

I don't know how to explain to Roman that it's all tied together for me—as though it's Bonnie herself who's squeezing the air out of my father's lungs. As if all that she's taken from him already wasn't enough.

'It's… hard to explain.'

Roman nods but without meeting my eyes. He puts his water glass down.

'Lottie,' he begins, then stops.

I look at him.

'I've been thinking about something.' He fiddles with the sheet. 'I was thinking I might stay in Birch Bend next year.'

'But you're taking a gap year,' I say. He hasn't booked his flights yet, but I know he's planning to be gone by Christmas, spending winter backpacking somewhere warm.

He looks at me. 'I was going to.'

His searching tone puts me on edge.

'And now you want to stay *here*?'

He frowns. 'You sound disappointed.'

I look away. 'It's just, this isn't the plan. You're supposed to… I don't know, travel the world. Go to Machu Pichu or Patagonia or somewhere. Bungee-jump off things.'

He doesn't smile. 'And you were supposed to move down to Poughkeepsie and start training to be a chef…'

'I *can't*,' I say sharply. 'You can still go do the things you want to do. You can't just stay here and work in a bar for the rest of your life.'

He blinks.

'Does it bother you that I work in a bar?'

I feel irritable. This isn't how it was supposed to go.

'It's a student job. You're a student.'

His face tightens. 'No. I *was* one until last month. Right now I'm a guy who works in a bar.'

'It's not about your job,' I explode. 'I don't care what you do, Roman. I'm just saying you're younger than I am, and… you're *young*.'

He crosses his arms.

'Lottie. You're three years older than me. Not thirteen. Three.'

I look away.

'Is that what's really at the heart of this?' he goes on. 'You can't take me seriously because I'm not some older guy?'

'No,' I say, but inside part of me is saying *yes*. I guess I've only ever pictured myself with older guys, if I'm honest. Like Nico, my college boyfriend who was four years older than me. I liked how he was a few steps ahead, always ready to show me what he'd learned about the world. He wasn't always that much fun I guess, but he always knew what he was doing. He made sure I never had to worry about anything.

Roman's voice is cooler now.

'You know, Lottie,' he says. 'When I met you you told me how you felt you couldn't be a grown-up in your regular life. That you were stuck being the baby in the family and you wanted to break free of all that. But that ex of yours you've told me about—'

'Nico,' I mutter.

'It sounds to me like he just treated you like a baby-doll, too.' He looks at me. 'I don't see what the point is of breaking away to be somebody's baby-doll instead of somebody's baby daughter.'

'I was not a *doll*,' I snap.

But a little voice pokes at me. *Weren't you?*

Roman frowns. 'I can't make you take me seriously, Lottie. But I hope you can see that I treat you like the real, grown woman you are. Don't sabotage me because of it.'

My head aches. I want to snap something sharp back at him but nothing comes out.

'I don't think I can think about all this right now,' I say.

Roman nods as I leave the room. He doesn't walk me to the door. He doesn't kiss me goodbye.

Chapter Fifteen
Dinah

Max leans in to kiss me as I sit in the passenger seat.

'Radio?' he asks, and Josie perks up a little when he puts on her favorite station. I squeeze his hand on the transmission, and he squeezes back.

He texted me this morning saying he was sorry about how we left things last night. I can admit, we were both tired and not at our best. So when he proposed checking out a house this afternoon that had apparently just gone on the market, I felt we should give it a shot. I'm maybe not in the best head-space but Max is so sure it'll be a good distraction for me, and I know he's got this idea that I'm not as excited as he is about our future. It's just that that future is so overshadowed right now.

Meanwhile, Jeff asked if he could take Josie by the McCrae house for dinner tonight; he's grilling, apparently.

It's maybe a thirty-minute drive to the place Max spotted on his real-estate app, and when we pull up outside, I suck in a breath. It's nice. *Really* nice. One of those sharp modern constructions with huge windows. I wonder if we can afford it—Max is making more than I am but his business is still pretty new.

I look in the rearview mirror and see Josie's dazzled look.

'What do you think, Jojo?' I say.

'Who lives here?' she says.

'Well, no one.' Max turns. 'It's new. We'd be the first.'

I can see her turning that over in her mind. I do too. How strange to be in a house with no history. Strange... but liberating.

We walk up the perfect flagstones through the perfect yard, to the perfect front door. It opens smoothly and silently, not sticking and creaking in the humidity like we're used to.

Inside it's almost cool, even though the AC's not on and it's summer.

'Energy-efficient design,' Max says.

And I have to admit it's beautiful. Everything is tasteful, sleek, pristine.

'Wow,' Josie says.

'Do you like it?' I turn to her.

She nods. 'Can I go upstairs?'

Max agrees. 'Go pick out your bedroom,' he says, and her eyes widen.

'Careful on those stairs,' I say. They're the 'designer' kind, no runner laid down to stop a nasty fall.

'I will!' Josie scampers up them and disappears.

Max looks at me, not wanting to ask. And I feel nervous. Despite how beautiful it is, it's all so different to what I'm used to.

Then he leads me into the kitchen.

'The garden,' I say, because it's immediately all I can think about. Half of one wall is glass, and through it all I see is green—beautiful, lush green. I imagine sitting here in the evenings, sharing a bottle of wine with Max after Josie's gone to bed, watching fireflies in the summer dusk. The flowers I could grow here.

Mom would have loved a garden like this, I think.

Josie comes flying back through the doorway, breathless.

'This place is amazing!' she says. 'Can we live here, Mommy? Can we?'

Max glances at me. The question's there in his eyes too, but there's something humble in them, like he's reminding himself not to push me, not to pressure me. He wants me to be happy.

I squeeze his hand.

'We'll see. But it sounds like a wonderful plan.'

*

Jeff drops Josie off only ten minutes later than he said he would. She has sauce on the corner of her mouth, and looks sated and happy. I put my hand on her tangled hair.

'Go wash up and get ready for bed,' I say. 'I'll come up soon.'

She bounces up the stairs and Jeff watches her go.

'Man, that energy,' he says.

'If we could bottle it, we'd be rich.'

He smiles. It's a familiar smile but it's different

than it used to be. I don't think it's just my imagination. There's traces of sadness in it. Of loss. I wonder if it's that loss that's made him want to rebuild things with Josie. It seems wrong that a realization like that should come at such a cost.

'So, how are you?' he says. 'Any updates on your dad?'

I think of our brief visit this morning. The machine breathing for him, that horrible, hissing exhale.

'He's on a ventilator,' I say. 'We're waiting. And hoping. It's… it's not looking great.'

'I'm sorry,' Jeff says.

I swallow. 'So Josie had a good time?'

He smiles. 'I hope so. She sure can eat.'

Despite myself, I laugh.

'She sure can.'

There's a pause then, a little awkward.

'Um, can I get a glass of water, Di?' he says. 'We walked over, and—'

'Of course.' I feel embarrassed. I open the door wider but he gestures to the porch swing.

'I don't need to come in, I can just wait out here…'

The swing always used to be Jeff's favorite spot. When I carry out two water glasses he stops swinging long enough for me to sit. The seat is big enough for three; I sit at the far end, leaving a body's worth of space between us.

'Thank you,' he says, and takes his glass.

We sip in silence. Jeff and I must have sat on this

same swing hundreds of times, telling each other our dreams, planning our futures. We were such kids.

'Di,' he says. 'I've been thinking. I know you have a lot to juggle, with the hospital visits to fit in on top of everything. What if I picked Josie up from school some afternoons next week? You could just let me know when you're back from work and I'll drop her over.'

I glance at him. I'm nervous about depending on Jeff—about treating him like a real co-parent—but it would be a help.

'I'll need to clear it with the school,' I say. 'They'll need a form.'

He nods.

'The view hasn't changed much from here,' he says after a while.

'It hasn't,' I agree.

The silence stretches.

'Do you remember,' Jeff says. 'How you used to call me "golden boy"?'

'Golden boy?' I look at him. Maybe I did call him that. I can imagine the sarcastic kind of tone I would have said it in. I always thought his mother idolized him too much—her only son, her youngest child.

He nods.

'You always said things came too easily to me. That I was born lucky.'

I feel awkward.

'Jeff—'

'You did,' he says. 'And you weren't wrong. I remember one time you said to me, *your problem, Jeff, is that nothing really bad has ever happened to you.*'

I look down at my hands. I'd like to deny it but it sounds true, like the kind of thing I would have said back then. I was so aware of what I'd lost so young.

I sip my water. Jeff *was* a golden child back in those days. But life is long, that's what I didn't realize then. Luck shifts like a tide. Sometimes, a tsunami.

I clear my throat. 'What was her name? Your girlfriend?'

He looks at me, weighing my question. I hope he can see that I'm asking out of respect and not some morbid curiosity. I guess he can, because his face relaxes and he turns back to the garden.

'Melody.'

Melody.

'That's a pretty name.'

For a while we both say nothing, then Jeff clears his throat.

'She was an outdoor tour guide,' he says. 'She'd lead hikes outside the city every weekend. She was from Oregon, originally. She loved the outdoors.' He glances at me. It's like he's been waiting to tell me—tell *someone*—about her.

'She wanted to move back to the West Coast,' he says. 'We were going to go out there, buy a little place. Somewhere quiet, out in the boonies.'

I frown. It sounds like a beautiful dream, but not

Jeff's dream.

'What would *you* have done?' I say.

He shrugs.

'I'd have picked up some gig, I guess. Or Mel and I talked about starting a tour agency together.' He looks at me. 'The music's just a thing. It doesn't have to be my life, you know.'

The music's *just a "thing"*?

I stare at him.

'But... but you were *always* on the road, Jeff. Music was your... your whole purpose.'

He doesn't look at me then. He just shakes his head.

'It wasn't, really. That was just what you always told me.'

I stare.

'What *I* told you? What are you talking about?'

He looks over.

'You said it pretty much since we met, Dinah: how I was going to be famous one day and it would kill our relationship; how I was going to end up picking the band over you. How music would always be my first love.'

I huff. 'I don't remember being that insightful at seventeen.'

'Well.' Jeff takes a swig of water. 'I think that depends on how you see it. I mean, if you say you just *predicted* the future, then it's like we never had a shot. But...' He clears his throat. 'But you know, Di, it can be hard to spend your days and nights constantly trying to prove someone wrong. Trying to prove to them that they can trust you. That you're not some fickle, flighty guy who's always on the verge of disappearing.' He cradles the glass in his hands. 'Sometimes it's easier to be on the road, driving around in that stinky van with your bandmates, where it's taken for granted that you're there because you want to be and you know in your bones you're a team.'

I cross my arms. I can't believe he's saying this.

'This isn't fair,' I say. 'You're blaming me.'

He shakes his head. 'I don't mean it that way. I'm sorry.'

'You were the one who kept leaving,' I go on. '*You* were the one who kept getting on that bus. You chose that, even though you knew you and I were falling apart.'

Or maybe because he knew we were falling apart, I think now.

'You're right,' he says. 'You're right, and that's on me. I was an adult. But… I was a very *young* adult, Di. We both were.'

I look back at him. I feel irritated, chastened…. and sad.

We sit, no longer swinging.

'Do you remember,' he says after a while. 'The first time I came up to visit? After we broke up, and you moved back?'

'I remember parts of it,' I say. Those were nightmare months, after I moved back from the city with a teething, sleepless two-year-old. I was grieving so hard. Mourning the loss of my future, the life that hadn't worked out. I remember that Jeff came up and stayed with his mom and we tried to make it a good weekend for Josie, but it all felt like a horrible charade.

'Mom just wouldn't stop,' Jeff goes on. 'She kept telling me how I'd messed up.'

That surprises me. I always thought Jeff's mom indulged him. But then I remember she's a single mom herself. She probably had some feelings of her own to work through.

'And the whole weekend,' Jeff continues. 'It felt so… it was awful, Dinah.'

'It was,' I say.

'I could feel how disappointed you were in me, and then Josie… it was the opposite. I felt like however badly I failed, whatever I did, she'd just look at me with those big eyes and forgive me on the spot.' He swallows. 'I don't know why that felt worse than anything else. It doesn't make sense, does it?'

But it makes a kind of sense.

'I didn't think I could handle it,' Jeff goes on. 'More and more visits like that. I just pictured years and years of that disappointment and guilt.'

I look at him.

'You're saying that's why you started flaking out all the time? Delaying your visits? Canceling on us?'

He looks at his hands.

'I'm not saying it was an excuse.'

'No,' I say, louder than I mean to. 'It wasn't. You didn't want to have to feel your feelings so you just stopped showing up, *despite* what that did to Josie's feelings.'

He swallows.

'You're right. It's not how I saw it at the time, but... you're right.'

I breathe out.

'I don't know what you want me to say, Jeff.'

'You don't have to say anything.' He looks at me. 'I didn't say this so you could make me feel better. I don't want to defend it—what I did and what I didn't do. I can't defend it. I just thought you deserved to hear.' He shrugs. 'For whatever it's worth.'

I cross my arms.

It's a lot to process. And if I'm honest it does make me sad—of course it makes me sad—to hear Jeff say such things. And yes, it makes me wonder. It was so hard at twenty-five, starting to see our future slip away. A future I later told myself was never meant to happen. And here's Jeff telling me it might have, should have. A tightness, a physical pain, swells in my chest.

But then I think of my daughter upstairs and I release the breath, I let the pain go. Because that's the beauty of life, isn't it? Its sheer, hard beauty: there's no such thing as backwards, only forwards. There's nothing to second-guess, because there are no do-overs. This alternate reality reaching out to me, whispering to me? It might look close, but in a world where time moves only one way, the past is behind a wall no one can pass through. Which makes it nothing more than an illusion, a will-o'-the-wisp. A beautiful piece of nostalgia that has nothing to do with the real me in the real world.

'I just want you to know, Dinah, that I want those good things for Josie too,' Jeff says. 'To be safe, happy... all the things you want for her. And I realize I haven't done much to give her those things, but you have. You really have.'

'Mommy!' A voice calls from inside then. '*Mommy!*'

It's a relief, in a way, to be done here.

I stand up.

'Sounds like I'm needed inside.'

Jeff nods.

'Goodnight, Dinah. And thanks.'

Josie's got her head buried in the last pages of *Prince Caspian*. I sit behind her, teasing out the tangles in her long, dark hair.

'Josie-bear, did you even attempt to brush this?'

'Yes,' she says defiantly. 'Only you brush it better.'

I lean into my daughter and the smell of her warm scalp. Jeff's words still linger.

I summon up the past, wish it peace, and push it out to sea.

After Josie's in bed I head back downstairs to the

living room, where Dad and Mara keep their old desktop. I'll print out that permission form for Jeff and have Josie give it to her teacher tomorrow. He deserves that much. So does she.

The monitor's dark but the minute my hand jogs the mouse it springs to life, and that's when I see it: my name.

I may not believe in snooping but my name's screaming out at me from the screen and my brain just can't help it. I'm looking at Dad's inbox, with the viewing pane open on a message.

From: **MatthewAtkins@AtkinsAssociates.com**.

Matthew Atkins. The lawyer who called for Dad.

And as I read on and my stomach turns to ice. I guess I make a noise, because suddenly Vaughan's in the room.

'What is it?' she says. 'Is it Dad? What is it?'

It is Dad.

Just not in the way she means.

*

Everyone's clustered around the screen. I want to push back my chair and escape from it all, run out of the house and find a forest to scream in.

This is what the email says:

Subject: Per our phone call.

George
As your lawyer I am prepared to execute the amendments to your will we discussed on our call.

But as your friend, if I may, I would invite you to reconsider. What you are proposing could drive a wedge between Dinah and her sisters forever. I have seen families estranged over less.

Nonetheless, upon your confirmation I am ready to proceed with your instructions.

Matty

I've read the message and reread it.

'He wouldn't,' Mara says again. 'Not without talking to me about it. He didn't *mean* it.'

The cold comes over me.

'Didn't mean what?'

She doesn't meet my eyes.

'He'd got it into his head that you were planning to marry Max. I thought he was being silly. But he was so sure, so convinced...' She shakes her head. 'When you told us, I wondered if somehow he'd known.' She hesitates. 'He wouldn't stop talking about it. You know he's never been a fan of Max or his family...'

I do know, but it hurts to hear it said like that. And I can feel there's worse coming.

'He was in a foul mood all of last week over it,' she goes on. 'Even the day of the party he was talking about it. I told him he had to get over it. That you were a grown woman, you'd make up your own mind.'

I startle. So *that* was what I overheard? Mara was... defending me, it sounds like.

'But he had this bee in his bonnet. He said at one point—' She takes a breath. 'I didn't think he meant it but he said he was going to contact Matty Atkins about it. About changing his will. That if you really did marry Max…'

I stare at her.

'He was going to cut me out?' I say.

Mara doesn't look at me. Neither of the others will meet my eyes either.

'You're serious. Cut me out of his will? Because I'm marrying someone he doesn't like?' I feel my vision blur. 'I mean, what *century* is this?'

Nobody moves, and I feel like I'm an animal in a zoo, the wary stares they're all giving me.

I can't believe it. I *won't*.

It's archaic. Tyrannical. It's not like Dad.

I look around the room, this house I've grown up in that holds so many layers of memories. We all know how Dad's will is supposed to go. Life rights in the house to Mara, then left jointly to us three girls.

My legacy. Josie's legacy. And now he wants to write us both out of it?

I can't believe it. But apparently I have to.

'He was going to talk to you, wasn't he?' Vaughan says. 'You said yourself. He was going to talk to you over the weekend about something. I bet he wasn't really going to change the will. He probably just wanted to use it to make a point. Try to talk you out of marrying Max.'

Vaughan sounds almost hopeful, like what she's suggesting is somehow more acceptable: that Dad didn't *really* intend to write me out of his will, it was just a bargaining chip, a way to manipulate me. But I think that might be worse.

Vaughan fixes her anxious eyes on me. 'And it doesn't sound like he actually got around to signing a new will. It's not valid.'

'It doesn't *matter* if it's valid yet,' I burst out. I slam a hand on the desk and my diamond winks back at me. I look down at it.

He knew, I think. *Somehow he knew.*

I feel Mara's eyes on me, and for a moment I think she's about to reach out and touch me. I stiffen. I feel electric with anger. With pain.

'Vaughan's right,' Mara says eventually. 'He didn't mean it. When he's back to his old self, when he's home… you and he can talk this through. It'll sort itself out.'

I close my eyes.

I'm too old for bedtime stories.

'Excuse me.' I stand up. I can hear the ice in my voice; the ice that's wrapping around my ribcage. 'I think I need some air.'

*

As I walk the neighborhood I keep my hands by my sides balled in fists, the way I learned to do as a teenager when I was trying to keep my feelings in check. Daddy and Mara used to tell me not to "act out," but I struggled to understand how people could feel the things I felt and not show it. And right now what I'm feeling is that I want to hit something. I want it to hurt. I want the bruise.

This can't be the way I say goodbye to my father.

Right through our childhoods Dad always talked about loving all of us equally, how his three daughters were the most precious things to him. If he bought something for one of us he'd find a way to treat each of the others, so we never had grounds to bicker.

The phrase *cut off* echoes in my head. Cut like scissors. Like a guillotine. That thread that binds me to my past—the golden thread that goes back to Mom, to before I was born. There it goes.

Snip.

How will I ever tell Josie about this?

How will I ever tell Max?

George

Waves are lapping somewhere. George blinks in the dark. Is this some sort of beach he's lying on? He's not in the water any more. It seems to have washed him up here, on some dark shore. George stares up into the blackness overhead. Shouldn't there be stars?

The silver apples of the moon, a voice says, smiling.

That old, remembered voice.

There's something itching at him, something that's trying to make its way into his mind. If only he could remember what it was.

There's somebody waiting for him.

Something he needs to explain.

A story that needs telling.

A wrong that needs righting.

Home, he thinks. But he doesn't know how to get there from here. He doesn't know the way. He has no guide.

He looks up into the blackness again.

Stars, he thinks. There should be stars. If only there were stars.

Chapter Sixteen
Lottie

'Can I come in?'

Mom looks up from where she's perched on the side of the bed. The bed looks huge, Dad's empty side like a reminder. She's got something in her hand which she pushes to the side, almost guiltily.

'Come in, Lottie.'

'I can't get my head around it.' I drop onto Dad's side of the bed. 'Did he really say all that about changing his will?'

Mom sighs. 'I thought he was just blustering, Lottie. I don't know what got into him.'

Nor do I. It seems so out of character.

'I know he doesn't like the Brannaghs, Mom. But this whole thing—it's way out of proportion, isn't it?'

Mom shakes her head.

'It is. But I suppose it's an old resentment, and those are the ones that go deepest. Bonnie died so soon after that restaurant kerfuffle. I think it all fused together a bit for your father.'

'He should have gotten over it.' I shake my head. 'And how could he expect to change Dinah's mind? I mean, this is *Dinah*.'

Mom sighs heavily. Her gaze moves to the window. 'They're so alike in some ways, she and

George.'

'You think so?' I've always kind of assumed Dinah was like her mother.

Mom looks back at me.

'Well, they're both bull-stubborn, for one thing. And those fierce hearts.'

I think of Dad's heart, fierce maybe but also weak.

'You remember when she was a teenager, Lottie?' Mom shakes her head. 'Your father and I argued about her constantly. We never argued about anything; only Dinah.' She looks at me. 'It drove me crazy, you know, how I could never seem to be the bigger person with her. I knew how much she'd lost, and yet somehow it was like she knew the *exact* right thing to say to drive me crazy. I thought, what kind of woman wants to lash out at a motherless teenager? I didn't lash out, of course... but I *wanted* to.'

'But you didn't,' I say. 'Even though you wanted to.'

I feel like we're moving into unfamiliar territory. This isn't the kind of thing Mom and I talk about.

Mom sighs. 'She's not always easy, your sister, but she is remarkable.'

I nod, and I'm surprised to feel just a hint of jealousy.

'She'll still marry Max, won't she?' I say.

Mom looks at me.

'I'd say now more than ever. Dinah always defends the underdog, you know.'

She's right. Dinah would always protect me when

192

I was little, just like she protects Josie now. Anybody who's vulnerable, she wants to stand in front of. And I guess Dad *has* made Max into an underdog now.

It feels strange to talk about this stuff with Mom. We never talk about our family like this. We never talk about *anything* like this. Sometimes I think Mom got so used to parenting stepdaughters—to giving them "space"; to not trying to act like their mother for fear of them shouting back, *you're not my real mom*—that she didn't know how to course-correct when I came along.

So many things in my life she doesn't know how I feel about. And so many things about her I don't know either. Her choices. Her feelings. Her regrets.

'Mom?' I say after a while.

She looks at me.

'Did it ever bother you, that you weren't Dad's first wife?'

It's clear from her face this wasn't what she was expecting.

'I mean…' I swallow. My throat feels suddenly dry. Maybe we're not ready for this conversation. 'Do you ever hate this house, how it was hers first?' I look down at my hands. 'How *everything* was hers first?'

Mom says nothing. My words hang in the air, embarrassing me. Finally I look at her but I can't make out her expression. It's pained, and somehow private.

'Come up here,' she says eventually. She slides something off the nightstand, the thing she put away as I came into the room.

I hesitate, then slide up to sit beside her. She hands it to me. It's a family photograph—not of our family, but of *her* family. It looks like it was taken in maybe the sixties. I look into the youthful faces of my grandparents. Grandpa's got Mom on his lap, and Grandma...

'Wait,' I say. 'Who's the other kid?'

Because there are two little girls in the photo. Now that I'm looking between them I can't even tell which one is Mom. But she's an only child.

Mom exhales slowly.

'I had a sister. When I was very young.'

My mind whirls.

'Her name was Charlotte.'

The breath rushes in so fast it stings my lungs. *Charlotte.* No one's ever called me by my full name. I've always been Lottie.

'What happened to her?' I ask. I know; of course I already know. But I still need to hear it.

'She died.' Mom's voice sounds detached, far away. 'She had a heart defect. It wasn't diagnosed. If it had been, they could have saved her.'

'How old was she?' I say. My voice comes out so hushed I barely hear it.

'She was almost two when she died,' Mom says. 'I was three.' She goes on. 'I can't remember her, you know. I mean, sometimes I think I can, but I can't tell if I'm imagining it. My parents never talked about her.' She looks at me. 'They sealed themselves off from it completely. I know Dinah likes to say I'm an Ice Queen—'

I flush. I didn't know she knew that.

'—But if she'd grown up with my mother...' Mom trails off. 'I suppose Mom and Dad were just doing what they could to survive. I suppose we all were.' She shuts her eyes. 'I just always felt so guilty, not being able to picture her face.'

She shrugs, like she won't let herself off the hook. Like she's *supposed* to be able to remember.

I set the photo down gently on the bedspread. We both look at it.

'You know,' Mom says, 'I think that was part of why your father and I understood each other. I knew what it was to feel you'd failed someone—that you were the one left behind and that you weren't enough.'

I don't know what to say. I'm thinking about my sisters, and about Charlotte. About Bonnie and Dad. And Mom. I look at her looking at the photo, and I wonder if some tiny part of her is angry at her sister for dying and leaving her all alone in that sad house.

I wonder if that anger is why she still feels so guilty all these years later.

We sit, and the room seems to throb quietly around us.

Ice Queen.

I take in the pale walls, the white furnishings,

everything as blank and clean as an iceberg. It isn't unfriendly, I realize then. It isn't hostile. It's just therapy. It's waking up every morning to a fresh start. To a place where the past doesn't cling to you.

I think of Grandma and Grandpa's house, the occasional times we've flown to Indiana to see them. When I think of their house, I think of silence. And not a calm silence like when old friends sit together, but the kind of dutiful silence you get when everyone's paying too much attention. Tiptoeing around each other and trying not to make a noise.

Maybe if old wounds never heal, you never stop tiptoeing—because you know that even something small can slice you open all over again and the pain will be there still.

Mom looks back at me, and her mouth pulls into a sad little half-smile.

'I don't mind that this house holds memories of Bonnie, Lottie,' she says. She shifts her weight. 'I want your father to remember her. It's a gift, being able to love who you've lost. I envy him that, but I wouldn't wish it away from him.' She clears her throat. 'Was it hard sometimes? Yes. Even to me,' she goes on. 'Your father rarely spoke about Bonnie. It used to hurt that he was so private. I suppose men are raised to be private with their pain.'

But not just men, I think.

'I'm really sorry,' I say at last. 'About your sister.'
She nods.

'We all struggled in our ways.' She pauses. 'I think

Mom was depressed for a long time after Charlotte.' She looks at me. 'I used to wish so much we could get out of the house. Go places. Do things. But she never really had the energy. I never got to do the stuff my schoolfriends did—youth groups, swimming lessons, music, tennis. I wanted it all so much.'

I look at her. What she's saying is resonating uncomfortably for me. I don't know why at first.

'I remember feeling like there was no *air* in the house anymore,' she goes on. 'That I just needed to be somewhere else. Anywhere with people, noise.' She stops. 'I hated that house, Lottie. I hated coming home from school at the end of the day.'

I think we're both startled for a moment. Such frankness isn't something we're used to. And as I think about her words something takes root in my mind.

'Mom…' I say tentatively. 'Is that… is that why you signed me up for so much stuff when I was a kid?'

Because I, too, sometimes felt like I couldn't breathe. But I felt it in a different way. I don't have enough fingers to count all the extracurriculars I did back then: flute lessons, basketball, badminton, gymnastics… pottery, tap, soccer, track. I could go on. It felt like there was something new I was being pushed towards every year, and I always wanted approval so I always did it. I brought home the medals, the certificates, and it seemed to make Mom happy, or at least happier, so I kept doing it. I brought home more and more medals so that someday something would crack open and we could, I don't know, *laugh* together. Become the kind of mother and daughter I saw on TV.

I look up and Mom's looking at me. So carefully.

'Sweetheart,' she says. Her voice is gentle. I feel myself tearing up and I don't want to. She sucks in her breath and puts a hand on mine.

'I just wanted you to be happy,' she says. She pauses. 'I wanted you to have the things I didn't.'

'Mom—'

She shuts her eyes. 'I didn't want you to feel like a prisoner, and start to hate your home... hate *me*.... the way I...'

I shake my head. 'Mom... how could I hate you?'

She just looks at me.

I remember Dinah's raised eyebrows as over the years I would be piled into the car for yet another basketball practice, yet another ballet lesson.

'I don't get it,' I say. 'You kept me out of the house to, what, "protect" me from you? I saw my basketball coach more than I saw you!'

Mom flinches.

'But... you *liked* Ms. Rahul,' she says. But I see my words sinking in even as she protests.

And yes, she's right, I liked my coach. I liked my music teacher too. I liked my teammates and my bandmates, and I developed my skills, and I got into a good college because of my full-to-bursting "all-rounder" resumé. None of it was *bad*. But none of it was the thing I wanted most.

The truth is it wasn't even about time. It wasn't that I needed a mother who was always around, permanently on call. It was just that...

'The thing is,' I say, but I don't know how to describe it, that feeling that even when she was there, sometimes she wasn't *there*.

'You remember sometimes when it was just the two of us?' Those times were rare enough in my childhood, when Mom and I had an hour or two to ourselves, when Daddy and Dinah and Vaughan were somewhere else and the house was empty. 'Do you remember,' I say, 'how you'd get up and put the radio on?'

She looks at me, and I can see she's trying to understand what I'm struggling to say. I see the very beginnings of it sink in.

'I just...' I stop. 'I wish it had been more comfortable for you to be alone with me.'

There's a silence then.

It stretches.

'Oh, Lottie.' Mom says it so quietly, and I have to push tears away.

'I love you more than anything,' she says. 'From the second you were born. It almost killed me how much I loved you—I'd never had a feeling that big. And there were just so many ways to be scared.' She pauses. 'I worried I would let you down; or that I'd turn you against me somehow, or that I'd smother you with too much love. If I ever held back—if you ever felt I was keeping my distance—it was just that I wanted you to grow up… free.'

I look at her, and she looks back at me.

Freedom.

Our country is obsessed with that word.

But sometimes I wonder if we even really know what it means.

*

For the first time in a week, I fall asleep without tossing and turning. When I wake it feels late, sun streaming in the windows. I push my feet into slippers. *Saturday.* A week since the party.

Vaughan's brewing coffee, fully dressed and pristine as usual.

'Want a cup?' She turns her big grey eyes on me and I think of Dad's little nickname: *silver girl.*

'Thanks,' I say. I hesitate. 'Have you seen Dinah this morning?'

Vaughan shakes her head, looking awkward too.

'She and Josie must have gone out early.'

Avoiding the rest of us, no doubt.

Vaughan pulls two mugs from the cabinet and takes milk from the fridge.

I'm not sure if it's been just the two of us alone in the room since she's come home. Looking at the deep hollows under my big sister's eyes, I want to ask her how she's doing, how she's *really* doing, but I know she'd just nod and say something stoic. Vaughan doesn't really show weakness. I think back to last night... then again, maybe no one in this family does. I guess Dinah's the only one who really wears her heart on her sleeve, not that that's always worked out for her. The rest of us, well... we keep our secrets to ourselves.

I swallow.

My own secret is something I forget most of the time... and then suddenly something will remind me, and I'll look at my eldest sister and the guilt comes flooding back.

I glance at her tired eyes again as she passes me a mug. Super-competent Vaughan. Vaughan of the Perfect Life. Surely nothing can derail that. But still...

'Vaughan?' I say.

She looks up.

'Is everything... I mean, nothing's okay right now, I know that. But.... are you doing okay?'

She meets my eyes, and her face softens. It's like she's debating something before she finally shakes her head.

'Yeah. I'm okay, Lottie. Thanks for asking.' She checks her watch. 'I'm about to drive over to the hospital. You want me to wait?' She looks at my pajamas and slippers.

'It's okay,' I say. 'I'll go in later.'

There's something I want to do first. Not the kind of thing I can tell Vaughan about.

'If you're sure,' she says.

She drains her mug and puts it in the sink, then goes out to the hall. I hear her rooting around out there.

'Lottie, can you see my purse in there?'

I scan the surfaces and call back a no.

She's back upstairs when her cellphone starts ringing.

'Vaughan! Your phone!' I call. I move to where the phone's lying on the kitchen table and see the name flashing up.

Mitchell. Of course.

'Pick up for me?' Vaughan hollers from upstairs.

My stomach turns. I hesitate, then hit accept.

'Vee—' Mitchell's voice comes down the line.

'Hi, Mitchell, it's Lottie,' I interrupt. My stomach roils again. 'Vaughan's just gone upstairs. She'll be down in a second.'

'Oh, hey Lottie,' Mitchell says easily. 'Thanks. And, hey, I'm so sorry about what you're all going through.'

'Thank you,' I say. It sounds like he means it. Even narcissists feel sympathy, right?

Vaughan clatters back downstairs, purse over her shoulder, and holds out her hand.

'I'm passing you back to Vaughan now,' I say.

Thank you, she mouths as she takes the phone from me. But there's something else in her body language now, a brittleness that wasn't there before.

'Mitch?' she says, and plucks keys from the bowl by the door. I watch her leave, and tell the feeling in

202

my stomach to settle down. I take another swig of coffee to settle it but it doesn't help.

And then a thought hits me. I look at the wall calendar, do a quick mental calculation.

I'm not *that* late. And anyway, I've never been one of those girls that's regular as clockwork. It's probably nothing.

*

I got the address online, but once I pull up I just sit for a while, wondering if I should turn the car around and go straight home. A lone kid shimmies up and down the street on his skateboard and a sickly-looking pit bull on a chain lies in the sun nearby.

I lock the car and walk slowly to the front door of number 158. The man that answers looks me up and down.

'Well, you're not selling Girl Scout cookies, are you?'

I clear my throat.

'Mr. Cahill?'

He frowns harder.

'Yes?'

'Mr. Cahill, hi. I'm Lottie Spencer. My father is George Spencer...' I wait to see if I'll get a reaction, and I do. It takes a moment, but then his eyes widen.

'You're Bonnie's girl?'

I hadn't expected that.

I shake my head. 'I'm not her daughter. But I was hoping I could speak with you about her. About

Bonnie.'

Mikey Cahill blinks. His face turns skeptical.

'Wait, did George send you down here? If your daddy has something left to say to me after all this time, he can damn well come down here and say it himself—'

'No,' I jump in. 'Nobody sent me, Mr. Cahill. I just wondered if I could talk to you. Just for a minute.'

He stares at me for a while, then turns and disappears down the hallway. I hesitate, trying to decide if it's an invitation to follow. One way to find out.

The hallway leads to a little kitchen that overlooks a scraggly back yard. Mikey Cahill fills a glass of water from the sink.

'So,' he says. 'What is it you want to know?'

I resist the urge to put my hands behind my back like a nervous child.

'I heard you and Dad used to be friends. And that you had a falling out, after Bonnie died.'

'Well, that's hardly news,' he says.

'It is to me.' I clear my throat. 'My father doesn't talk much about those days.'

'Is that so?'

Mikey puts down the water glass and comes my way. He leans towards me and I force myself not to shrink back. But then I see he's pointing to his forehead, a spot above his temple with a small, white scar.

'Your daddy did that,' he says. 'Came right at me.

Got me with the side of his wedding ring.'

I stare at the small scar. My dad did that? When Andrea said there'd been a 'falling out' I didn't picture, well, a *brawl*.

'So, what happened?' I say, wondering if he'll admit to an affair with Bonnie right out.

Mikey sighs.

'Well, it was all about the car, wasn't it. If I hadn't been out sick that week...' He shrugs, like the rest is obvious.

'What car?' I say.

His forehead puckers, like he doesn't understand why I'm being so slow.

'*Her* car, Bonnie's car, of course. That old jalopy she refused to give up on.' He looks at me. 'She picked it up from the garage maybe a week before the accident. So afterwards, your dad just couldn't let it go. Kept asking himself if he'd missed something. Thinking maybe if he'd done a better job, what happened wouldn't have happened.'

My mouth feels dry. I can't believe I've never heard this part.

'There was something wrong with her car?' I echo.

And Dad missed it? The irony is too terrible.

Mikey shakes his head.

'No one found any suggestion that the car was faulty. Even the coroner's report found nothing about the car. And besides, your dad was a perfectionist. He always checked everything twice. There was no way he let any car—least of all *her* car—out of his shop in anything less than roadworthy condition. But that wasn't the point. Your dad was convinced all the same that he should have spotted something. Couldn't shake the doubt.'

I digest that.

'But then... why did he blame you?'

Mikey Cahill crosses his arms. 'Well, I was out that week and he was short-staffed. Trying to do the work of two men instead of one.' He sighs. 'I struggled a lot with my drinking back then.' He looks around the kitchen as if imagining where else he might be, had things been different. 'I never meant to leave your dad high and dry, but it happened some days. He just dealt with it. But then in hindsight, I guess he felt like if he'd had the backup on that one day, things might have been different—he might've seen something.'

Wow.

'And you've never spoken since?' I say finally.

'Nope.' Mikey raps the side of the kitchen counter as if to say, *the end*.

I guess I had it all wrong. His falling-out with Dad wasn't about an affair. But then I remember Andrea the waitress's comment—how Mikey used to come to the restaurant for lunch almost every day. I figured it was because he had a crush on Bonnie.

'Did you know her well?' I say. 'Bonnie?'

He sighs, shrugs.

'I went to high school with her. She was the one who introduced me to George, got me the job at his garage.'

'You went to that restaurant where she worked a lot, right?'

He looks bemused for a minute.

'Yeah, there was a girl there I was pretty sweet on.'

Oh.

'So you and Bonnie…' I say. 'You were never…you know, a couple.'

He scoffs.

'Me? She wouldn't have looked twice at me. Not that she was my type either, to be honest. Easy to fall for, less easy to live with, that's what I figured.' He leans back against the counter. 'She was one of those people that are always dialed all the way up, you know? A little wild.' He pauses. 'I'm not saying it wasn't an absolute tragedy, of course it was, but I guess it didn't totally surprise me when I heard about the accident.'

'How do you mean?'

He blinks at me.

'Her driving.'

I frown, and he shakes his head.

'Your dad's kept you in a bubble, all right.' He coughs. 'She was speeding pretty bad, they said,' he goes on. 'They could tell from the angle of impact. The road was closed for resurfacing, too, but she went right through the sign. I guess in the dark and speeding like she was, she just didn't see it.'

I feel dazed.

'You'd think if the tar was wet it should have

slowed her down,' he goes on. 'Maybe it did at first. But pretty soon that stuff gets all up in the treads, gums 'em up. No grip left in the tires.'

The nausea in my stomach returns, and I feel a rush of bile in the back of my throat.

'You okay, kid?' Mikey Cahill eyes me.

'I'm fine. Thank you.' I swallow, smooth back my suddenly sweaty hair. 'I think I—I just need to go.'

I see Mikey Cahill's silhouette in my rearview as he stands in his open doorway, watching me leave. The pit bull turns its rheumy eyes as I start the engine. I pull out, glancing back before I round the bend. The road is quiet, motionless in the sun. It might as well be a ghost town.

Chapter Seventeen
Dinah

'Mommy?' Josie eyes me from her bar stool at the kitchen island as I slice a sandwich for her lunch. 'Are you still going to marry Max even though Grandpa doesn't want you to?'

I put down the knife, very carefully.

'How do you know about that?'

She shrugs.

'I heard Auntie Vaughan and Grandma talking. Why doesn't Grandpa want you and Max to get married?'

I don't answer for a moment. I don't know how.

'Well, baby,' I say finally. 'That's a question that only your grandpa can really answer.'

'But will you?' she says. '*Will* you marry him even if Grandpa doesn't want you to?'

She sounds... disapproving. And it's a strange sensation to feel disapproved of by your seven-year-old child. I raise my eyebrows at her.

'Do you always do what I want you to, Jojo?'

She looks somberly at me.

'Yes,' she nods.

'Well, don't,' I say. 'Not when you're a grown-up, anyway. Sometimes in life we need to make our own decisions.'

She licks peanut butter off the back of her thumb.

'Do you love Max, Mommy?'

I don't know what my face is showing. I turn away from her, pushing the jelly back into the fridge.

'Of course,' I say. But when I look back her level gaze is still there. I sigh.

'Josie... We've talked about this. You like Max, right? And you're okay with this? If Max and I get married?'

She looks back down at her sandwich, pushes a piece of crust to one side.

'Yeah.'

I tossed and turned all night, having conversations with Dad in my mind. Not one of them helped. No matter what Mara or Vaughan says about him "not being himself," I don't understand how he could have left us in this situation—not just me but the granddaughter he adores. Thinking about it feels like holding broken glass in my hand, and I try not to let its sharp edges touch me. I look out over the front yard, the creep of orange early-morning light on the grass.

Dad loves his garden. The rockery and herb garden and trellis of climbing plants at the back. The carefully tended lawn and Mom's magnolia at the front. He's given it the best of himself for decades. *Nature's my cathedral, Dinah.* He used to say that to me when I was little, "helping" him outside with my watering can. I've seen him out there so often, mowing, weeding, watering, trimming... and then when all the work is done, just striding along the beds inspecting them, nodding at his handiwork—or else reclining in a lawn chair, listening to Charlie Parker or another of his jazz greats on his straight-from-the-80s headset.

I picture the garden without him, slowly wilting, turning brown and thorny and overgrown. Angry and sad.

'Mommy?'

I look at Josie.

'I want to visit Grandpa.'

I swallow. I told myself if things got to a certain point I would offer Josie the chance to say goodbye. But unless or until then I figured I'd just keep her away from the whole experience. Those rooms, the fear and pain you can almost smell when you walk through those corridors.

'He doesn't look good right now, Jojo. He has lots of tubes going into his nose and throat to help him breathe.'

'That's okay.'

I shake my head. 'He wouldn't know you're there.'

She frowns.

'How do you know he won't know?'

'I mean because he's asleep,' I say, but I realize she knows that. She just believes he'll know, all the same. And who am I to contradict her?

'Are you sure, baby?' I say. 'I don't want you to be scared.'

She looks at me.

'You always tell me it's okay to be scared.'

I push her hair back from her face.

'I guess I do.'

'Are *you* scared?' she says.

'Yes,' I say finally, and she sits with that for a while.

'Did Grandpa used to hold your hand when you were scared?' She looks up at me. 'When you were a little girl?'

I nod.

'Me too,' she says. And I realize she's telling me that those days are past: not because her grandpa isn't here, but because she's not a little girl any more.

And my heart breaks just a little bit more.

*

I tell Josie to wait in the Family Room for a minute and that I'll come back and fetch her. I just want to check that nobody's in the middle of changing a drip or a catheter or anything. But then outside Dad's room I pause. The privacy curtain isn't drawn all the way round, and through the gap I see Mara at Dad's bedside. I thought she'd finished visiting this morning.

At first I think she's stroking his face, but then I see the razor in her hand. She's angled herself carefully over Dad, slowly shaving off that stubble he would hate.

I stand frozen, watching her guide the razor over his cheeks. Can he feel it? Is the pressure too hard, too soft? When Mara stands back from the bed I see the shake in her shoulders. But she doesn't turn and see me. I think about what it would take to go in there and put an arm round her, the way Lottie might. But I doubt that's something I'll ever be able to do.

And then from out here I see her start, and when she moves away I see the tiniest red speck bloom under Dad's chin. She's nicked the skin. In that moment I hate her; I really hate her. But then I see her face and the pain in it. I see how her hand trembles as she puts her thumb to the tiny speck of red and keeps it there, applying pressure.

I turn and walk away.

'Your grandma's visiting right now,' I tell Josie. 'Let's give her some time alone.'

Josie threads a piece of her hair between her lips and chews on it.

'Is Grandma scared too?' she says.

I clear my throat.

'Yes, baby. I think she probably is.'

*

Max and I are eating the dinner he's brought over. Josie's done eating and has gone to the living room. Our visit went okay, I guess. She asked some questions and stared a lot. I could feel how brave she was being and it hurt to be there with her, but I was proud in a way, too.

'Max?'

He spears a forkful of salad and looks up at me. I take a breath.

'You didn't say anything to my dad, did you? About us getting married?'

One thing I can't understand is how Dad *knew*. It sounds like the week Max proposed, Dad was suddenly expecting it.

Max frowns.

'Me? When would I have done that?'

'I don't know,' I say. 'I just wondered.'

'I didn't think you were the type to want me to ask his permission first. Did you want me to?'

I shake my head and Max goes back to his plate.

'Max?'

He puts down his fork this time.

'I don't really know how to say this.' I swallow. Right up until now I wasn't even sure I would tell him, but I feel like I can't sit on it any longer. And now that Josie's overheard the talk, she's liable to blurt something out that only makes it worse.

'I found out something,' I say, and take another breath. 'Dad... he really doesn't want us to get married.'

Max looks at me, baffled.

'But... why?'

I shake my head. 'It's not rational. I think he just feels protective of me—and Josie.' I don't go into the stuff about Max's family. This is hurtful enough to hear without making it more personal.

'He told you this?' I look at Max's face, the slight shake in his head like he can't quite believe I'm telling the truth.

'No.' I hesitate. But then I bite the bullet. I tell him about the email, the will.

I see the shock on Max's face as he computes what I'm saying. Guilt squeezes my chest, but then the hurt on his face turns cold.

'You barely invite me to things with your family. Is this why?'

I look down.

'I thought it would pass,' I say. 'Dad has his whims, but never like this. I guess after Jeff—'

'So he wants to lock you up in a castle? Never let another man near you?'

Max is right to be angry, but his tone makes me cringe.

'Even those times I've been *allowed* in this house,' he says bitterly. 'Your dad's been mostly gone, at the garage or something, even weekends. You told me he was just busy, always working.'

And he was. He just seemed to schedule that busyness when he knew Max would be coming by.

'I'm sorry,' I say.

He's silent for what feels like a long time.

'Well?' he says finally, and I look at him.

'Well?' he repeats. 'What are you going to do? Are you going to marry me? Or not?'

I can't believe he's asking me this.

'For goodness sake, Max. Is that really what you think of me? That this would make me change my mind?'

He turns away, something sullen in his shoulders.

'How should I know?' he says. 'It's not like I know where I stand with this family.'

'You know where you stand with *me*,' I say.

He grunts.

'You do,' I repeat.

'Well, that depends on a lot of things, doesn't it?' he says.

I cross my arms. 'Such as?'

'Where Jeff McCrae stands with you, for one thing.'

I close my eyes.

'Max,' I say. 'You have nothing to fear from Jeff. You really don't.' Of course it made me sad to hear Jeff say the things he said yesterday. But I know better than to let the might-have-beens play their little games with me. Why can't Max trust that?

'But Jeff *is* Josie's father, and it looks like maybe he's going to be around in her life again. And yes, I'm nervous about that but I won't lie: I'm happy about it if it's good for Josie.'

Max scoffs.

'"Josie."'

I frown.

'What's that supposed to mean?'

'Josie,' he says. 'You're always using her as your excuse, Dinah. Saying something's because of her because it's easier than admitting what you want.'

The words hit me like a blow. I stare at him, and the question races through my head: *Is he right? Am* I hiding behind my daughter? Pretending it's her I'm thinking of when it's really myself?

But then calmer thoughts flow back in like water settling, and I realize Max is wrong.

'Max.' I look at him. 'If I sound like I'm focused on Josie it's because I *am*. But don't tell me I don't tell you the truth about my feelings. I told you I would never play games with you and I meant it. When I needed time I *told* you I needed time, because I've assumed you trust me enough that I can speak truthfully, without you feeling insecure—'

He flares up.

'Insecure? You *make* me insecure, Dinah.' His voice rises. 'Damn it, Dinah, I'm your *fiancé*. I'm supposed to be first on your list.'

I look at him.

'I'm a parent, Max,' I say very quietly. 'Do you understand that? Do you really? Because that fact means you're not always going to come first. And if you can't understand that—' I don't know exactly how I'm going to finish that sentence but it feels big enough that I'm shaking.

'Oh, I understand,' Max says, getting to his feet. 'It's not like you've ever let me forget it.'

We look at each other for a moment, and then he shakes his head and walks inside. I pull myself to my feet and follow, but by the time I make it out the kitchen door he's already gone.

Chapter Eighteen
Lottie

I dream of Mikey Cahill that night. I'm in the ICU looking for Dad's bed, but I can't find him. When I finally get to the right bed, it's empty. There's just a man in a black suit turned away from me, head bowed like an undertaker. In the dream I freeze, and then Mikey turns around.

'Looking for George? You just missed him,' he says.

It's Sunday, and church bells are ringing outside.

Dinah's out early again. I only caught a flash of her last night, after Max stormed out of the house. I was standing on the stairs as he bolted out the front door, Dinah coming after him too late. She just stood there for a moment before she realized I was watching, then went inside to where Josie was watching TV and shut the door hard behind her.

Mom and I drive to the hospital; Vaughan said she'll come in later. Now I look at Mom standing at Dad's bedside, how washed out she looks these days. Her hair's got an inch of grey at the roots, something she'd never usually tolerate. The doctors have a crumb of good news for us, it turns out: Dad's lung function is better this morning than it was yesterday morning. But they make sure we know it's just a *crumb* of good news: without a steady trajectory one way or another, it's all just blips on a screen.

Outside, Mom stands in the parking lot looking dazed. She shakes her head.

'I can't remember where I parked the car.'

Mom, the one who always knows where every kitchen gadget is, whose every tax return has its own color-coded binder.

So I lead us down the rows of cars. Some are old and weather-beaten and some scream money, and I think how all their owners had to drive to the same sad place. Even the fanciest car can't protect you from whatever bad luck the universe wants to sling your way, I guess.

Mom tsks as she spots the car, and raises the clicker to unlock it. She glances at me as she buckles her seatbelt.

'Are you feeling okay, Lottie? You look a little pale.'

'I'm fine,' I say. Ignoring the faint nauseous feeling in my stomach.

I'm fine.

'I found out something,' I say when we hit our first red light. I take a breath. 'Bonnie... she was having an affair.'

Whatever reaction I was expecting, it's not what I get. Mom looks at me, sort of sadly.

'Have you said anything to your sisters?' she says.

I shake my head. 'Wait... Did you *know* about this?'

She sighs.

'Your father mentioned something once. It was a long time ago.' She eyes the stop light. 'I told you, even with me, he can be closed off about his life with Bonnie. But one night he'd... well, he'd drunk a lot, and he said something about an affair.'

So he did know.

Now I wonder how much.

'What did he say?'

Mom chews her lip.

'Well... that he'd found out about it, and she'd cried and sworn it was already over... and that they'd fought furiously about it all... and then a few weeks later there was the accident.'

The light turns green.

I sit, going over what Mom just said. How terrible that they were in the middle of fighting about it when the accident happened. Dad must blame himself for so much, even though it wasn't his fault. No one could have known.

'Who did she have the affair with?' I say.

Mom sighs. 'I don't know. I don't think your father ever found out that part. She called him "Clyde" apparently, whoever he was.'

'"Clyde"?' I say.

Mom purses her lips. 'Their little in-joke, it seems. That's how your father found out. I guess "Clyde" had been writing her these little love notes and your dad came across a stash of them.' She shakes her head.

Bonnie and Clyde. I close my eyes, feeling like an idiot. 'C' isn't Mikey Cahill, or a Charles or a Chris or a Calvin. C is anyone.

*My getaway girl—*that's what the note said. Another little joke.

'Let me out here?' I say at the next red light. 'I just want to walk for a bit.'

Mom looks at me. 'Here? You're sure?'

I nod.

'I can walk the rest of the way home.'

*

A call comes in on my cellphone as I leave the pharmacy. Roman. I take a breath and pick up.

'Hey.'

'Hey,' he says. There's silence.

'I shouldn't have said that,' he says. 'The other day. About your ex and all that.'

I tighten my grip on the handset.

'I guess you were right,' he says. 'About me not staying in Birch Bend. I mean, it doesn't really compare to Machu Pichu, right?'

Of course, I think. *Now you swing back around.*

'Lottie?'

'Okay,' I say curtly. 'Thanks for telling me.'

There's a pause.

'Lottie… do you want to talk about this?'

'What's to talk about?' I keep my voice hard. What does he want, applause for leaving?

'I just thought you might want to talk to me about it.'

'Well, I don't,' I say, as coldly as I can manage.

There's silence.

'Figures,' he says.

Figures?

'What's that supposed to mean?'

'That this is just like you.'

'You don't know me,' I say furiously.

'Lottie.' He takes a breath. 'I've been *trying* to get to know you ever since I met you. And I can't make you take me seriously, I can't make you see me the way I wish you would. But from what little you've let me learn about you from the last three months'—I hear him swallow and I know I won't like what's coming—'you have one sister you're practically estranged from and you've decided to just accept that, like it doesn't cut you to the core.' He takes a breath. 'You have parents who don't know what's going on in your world, to the point that they don't even know you're miserable in your job and fantasize about a new life. And… now that something really terrible has happened, you could be drawing strength from your family but instead you're on some wild goose chase about this dead wife of your dad's, like it's becoming some kind of vendetta for you.'

'It's not a *vendetta*,' I say through clenched teeth. But he goes on.

'It's like—it's like you think if you can just find answers to the past then the world will make sense again.'

I swallow.

'But *we're* the ones who make the world make sense, Lottie,' he says. 'Us, the ones who are still alive.'

His voice softens with the last words but it's too late. I'm done here.

'I'm going to go now,' I say.

'Lottie—'

'I'm going to go,' I repeat. 'Don't call me.'

I hang up before I start crying.

*

The house is empty. I come out of the bathroom with the stick in my hand.

It'll be negative. Of course it will. I've been careful, haven't I? The nausea I've been getting, it must be just stress.

The door slams downstairs. I check my watch. I'm sure from the tread, from the way she drops the keys into the bowl by the door, that it's Dinah. Josie's high voice sounds in the hall. They'll probably be upstairs in a minute. I step as quietly as I can to the attic staircase. In the attic I take a breath. I place the test carefully on the windowsill by the door. I hear the thump of a door below me and see Josie out at the side of the house, soccer ball under her arm.

Josie.

An amazing kid. A miracle, like all kids are.

But I can't have one. Not now.

Please not now.

I glance at my watch. How can it just be three

minutes that have passed? I'm wishing now I hadn't just snatched up the first test I found. I'd pay any money now to have the rapid-response kind.

Josie starts bouncing the ball off the wall outside. The not-quite-regular thump is like an itch I can't scratch. I cast my eyes around the room. Bonnie's boxes sit in the corner, looking back at me. I think of Roman going on about how we make our own meaning in the world, how we're the ones in control of our own destiny. I'll bet Bonnie thought that too, right up until her car ran off the road and her life got snuffed out like a match.

Roman thinks he knows everything. Well, he doesn't understand ghosts. Or the lengths we'll go to to get rid of them.

I think of Bonnie and fate and the way all our human stories twist up in each other's until no one can untangle one thread from another. Without Bonnie's death there would be no me: how does that even make sense? Does everything in life have to be at the cost of something else? It's terrifying to think we're all so connected, more than we even know. Because if we control so little, how can we ever keep anybody safe?

Your Clyde.

I guess Mom was right. Nothing will ever answer the parts I really want to know, like who Bonnie really was as a person, how much my father loved her, or why things happen the way they do.

Is this what Roman meant? That no matter how

much knowledge you collect, it'll never be enough? That it can't teach you the business of living or protect you from what's ahead?

'Lottie? What are you doing up here?'

I startle. I didn't even hear the door open.

'What are *you* doing up here?' I hit back.

Dinah shakes her head.

I feel tears of frustration prick behind my eyes. I just need her to go. *Now,* before she notices the pregnancy test propped up against the window ledge. The *thump, thump* of Josie outside with her soccer ball is like a mallet against my skull.

Dinah looks suspiciously at me, like she knows she'll find something here that's out of place.

'I just came up here for some peace and quiet,' I mutter.

I see her gaze travel to the boxes in the corner—the Bonnie boxes. And then it pans back around and stops.

'Lottie.'

Her eyes widen, and I feel my stomach turn over.

She's seen it.

She looks at me, then back to the test.

'Are you... are you... ?'

'I don't *know,*' I snap. 'Obviously.'

Eight more minutes.

She lets out a long breath through her teeth, and looks at me.

'What are you going to do?' she says. 'If—'

'I don't know that either,' I say miserably.

She looks at the test, then back at me.

'I'll go if you like,' she says slowly. 'But I can stay, if you want someone to wait with you.'

There's a pause. I think about telling her to go. I think about how I didn't expect her to stay.

I nod.

She closes the door.

We don't say anything for a while.

'What was it like for you,' I say finally, 'when you found out?'

Not that it's the same. Dinah was younger than I am now when she had Josie. But even if that pregnancy wasn't exactly planned, it was very much wanted.

Dinah sighs.

'I was scared, Lottie.' She moves to the front window, looking out over the driveway. 'The timing was... It was terrible, actually. I was so excited at first, and I was getting ready to tell Jeff. It was earlier than we'd planned but I was sure he'd be thrilled. And then...' She glances at me and I can't figure out the look in her eyes. It's bitter and sad and full of reproof.

'Then,' she says, 'I saw something one night. Something I'd never imagined I'd see. And I guess that's when I should have left him, instead of spending three more years trying to bury it, pretending what I'd seen wasn't the beginning of the end.' She sighs. 'But I was so scared that night—I was pregnant and I didn't want to be pregnant alone.

So I pretended I didn't know what I knew.' She looks down. 'I never thought I'd be the kind of person to lie to myself.'

My neck prickles. What did Jeff *do*?

'What happened?' I say. 'What did you see?'

She doesn't turn from the window.

'You're going to make me say it?'

'Say what?' There's a finger of dread plucking at me, something I don't yet understand.

'This is right where I was standing,' she says slowly. 'The night of your graduation party. It sounds silly, but I'd come upstairs to ask Mom's Magic 8-Ball a question. There's one of them in those old boxes of hers.' She crosses her arms, not looking my way. 'And I was standing right here, when I looked down and saw you two.'

I feel the blood rush to my face, to the roots of my hair.

So here we are, finally talking about it.

It took me months to understand that something between Dinah and me had truly broken—that it wasn't just her move to New York City, or the pregnancy, that was keeping her away and too busy to talk. I couldn't pin down when it had started—this cold war I didn't even know we were in—but over the months I eventually traced it back to the night of that party. That was the last night that everything had been fine… and then in the morning she was gone.

Then she'd shut me down so clearly that one time

in New York when I actually tried to bring it up. She was so fierce about it, and my stomach sank at her reaction because I knew then for sure: *she knew*. And if she knew, I couldn't blame her for not forgiving me. Loyalty is everything to Dinah and I had betrayed someone she loved. So I swallowed down my words and excuses. It hurt, but fighting would only have hurt more. And then instead of fighting, we built a wall.

'It should never have happened,' I say now. 'Never. But... I was only eighteen. *Barely* eighteen. I'd been drinking all night...'

Drinking *his* liquor. He'd been pouring, making sure my glass was never empty. I'd thought it was chivalrous.

'I know how old you were,' Dinah says coldly.

I remember being in the garden and realizing it was down to the two of us. My friends had left one by one, my sisters had gone to bed. I'd started to say goodnight, and then everything had veered in a different direction. By the time I realized the path we were on it seemed like everything was already too far advanced to stop it.

'Why didn't you tell Vaughan?' I say at last. 'If you knew?'

I should have told her myself, years ago. I just couldn't find the courage or the moment, and then it was too late.

Dinah turns from the window.

'I didn't tell *anyone*, Lottie,' she says. 'Because I

didn't want it to be real. I was humiliated and heartbroken and I put it down to the tequila and buried it in my mind as far down as I could.'

I shake my head. Denial I can understand, I tried it too. But *humiliated?* Heartbroken?

'Dinah,' I say slowly. 'Who did you think you saw out there with me, that night?'

Her eyes snap to mine, and for a moment she's very, very still. Then she shakes her head.

'Don't play games, Lottie. I know it was him. I saw his jacket.'

Memories flicker, a stitched-up patchwork of the night, the flashes I can remember. My friends mostly gone, a couple of the older guys smoking and cracking last beers on the side porch. Jeff passed out on the couch inside—I remember thinking it was sweet, the way he'd taken off his shoes first.

And Mitchell on the porch, putting on Jeff's left-behind jacket, the washed-denim one with all the patches. It wasn't cold—it was just an opportunity to mimic Jeff. I know I laughed at the impression. It wasn't hard to pull off—they had the same physique, same dark hair, and Mitchell was a good actor. I remember his eyes on me, enjoying the admiration, the laughter.

'Dinah, what you saw—what you think you saw… The guy was Mitchell. He was wearing Jeff's jacket. Jeff left it on the porch.'

And I'm back under the magnolia tree in the dark, Mitchell pulling me to him, my hands on his back, my fingers on the rough fabric, the satin liquid feel of the satin patches. I can smell it suddenly: the magnolia tree, Mitch's cologne.

Dinah's staring at me.

'*Mitchell?*' Her eyes are bugging out. 'Wait… *Mitchell?*'

'I'm so sorry.' I look away. 'I had no idea you thought…'

I trail off. Everything is through a different lens, suddenly. And I can only imagine how it feels for her.

'Was it… did you *want* it to happen?' Dinah asks.

It's hard to look at her when she asks that. I know she sees it in my eyes, how complex the answer is.

And I know why she's asking now, but never asked herself that when she thought it was Jeff. Jeff is shy. Mitchell is a leader.

I remember what a big deal everyone thought Mitchell was, how suave and accomplished. Or at least I thought they did. I remember how black the garden was. I remember how he whispered in my ear through the fog of moonlight and alcohol.

You're a lot more fun than your sister, aren't you?

It sent a shiver through me, a thrill of excitement and self-loathing mixed together. My back was right up against the tree, the rough bark digging through my shirt. I thought of pulling away at that point but I didn't have a picture of what that should look like. Heroines on TV pushed off lewd, repugnant attackers, maybe with a knee between the legs for good measure and a piercing cry for help. But this didn't look like that. This wasn't an attack.

Mostly, a little voice inside me says. *It* mostly *wasn't an attack.*

Let the record show, part of me *was* flattered. In my inebriated state, I felt a thrill. I felt grown up. I was eighteen and I'd never been kissed. With my million-and-one extracurriculars I'd hardly had a free second to even *talk* to boys.

Let the record also show: he was in his mid-twenties and I had just finished school, and he'd been pouring me drinks all night. And he had a man's strong body and I had a woman's.

It mostly wasn't an attack.

'A part of me wanted it,' I say. 'I think.'

'Oh, Lottie.' Dinah shakes her head. But I see now it isn't disapproval written on her face but sympathy.

If I could go back now to my eighteen-year-old self I'd tell her so many things. That she didn't need to be 'fun,' or anything else he told her she was. I'd tell her that there was no such thing as missing the moment to say no. That it was okay to make a boy angry. That saying no didn't mean things would get ugly.

Can you promise me that? I hear my eighteen-year-old self say. *Can you promise me it wouldn't have got ugly?*

I am almost sure—I am 90 percent sure—that Mitchell would have stopped if I'd told him to.

But not 100, my younger self whispers.

I didn't drink again for my first year of college. I put up with the other kids calling me Virgin Mary because I was alcohol-shy and boy-shy, and I figured that was just the price I paid for the mistake I'd made. If I got too drunk I'd start remembering Mitchell's hands traveling over me, going all the places I knew they shouldn't go.

'I figured you must have seen something,' I say finally. 'I figured you hated me because of what I'd done to Vaughan.'

Dinah shakes her head.

'Vaughan,' she repeats. 'She doesn't know?'

This part is hard for me. I swallow. 'I had just about gotten up the courage to tell her and then… they broke up. Do you remember? It was just a few weeks after that night. She said it was over.

'I figured I was off the hook … and then a few months later she came home and told us they were back together. That they'd worked it all out, they were moving in together…'

Vaughan had seemed so happy. She'd said Mitchell was like a 'whole new person,' that he'd been going through some tough personal stuff before, but he'd come through it and that everything was different now.

'So you never told her,' Dinah says quietly.

I can't quite meet her eyes.

'I couldn't bring myself to,' I say quietly. 'I felt sick when I thought about it. And I told myself it was just because they'd been going through such a rough patch. I felt like… if he *was* a whole different person now, I should just let the past be under the bridge.'

I used to imagine the way Vaughan would look at me if I told her. Not even anger, but something much worse.

Dinah absorbs what I've said.

'And since then? Mitchell, I mean…'

'He's been… perfectly civil,' I say. 'Perfectly appropriate.' I pause. 'You know, I think it's possible he's even forgotten that it ever happened.'

What a strange thing to think—that I've been carrying all this for years, but for Mitchell it's probably just an old scrap of memory floating in the outer reaches. Some people—some men, particularly—seem to have that gift, if you can call it a gift. Shame doesn't even seem to touch them.

'It's not like I've seen that much of him,' I add. It's always been a relief to me that Mitchell works so much, and Vaughan often comes home for the holidays alone.

Dinah looks at me and we're silent for a moment.

'It's not too late to tell her,' Dinah says finally. 'If you want to. If you think it's right.'

I'm kind of surprised that she's leaving the choice to me. That she's not insisting. I look at her face, all the anger drained out of it. She looks older, tireder. There's nothing but the *thump, thump* of Josie's soccer ball.

I guess Dinah sees my eyes flick back to the sill

then, because she clears her throat and looks that way too.

'Are you ready?' she says quietly.

I'm still asking myself that question when a yell echoes up from the garden. A man's voice.

I look at Dinah. Max's voice?

We hurry to the side window as the shouting goes on. The first yell was shock but now it sounds like words, and it sounds angry. The thrum of the soccer ball has stopped.

I look down and take in the scene: Max and Josie. Max in a crisp suit, mud all down his white shirt, an extravagant bouquet of flowers that he's cradling in his arms, now smashed and wilted. The football rolls away to one side.

'Is he shouting at *Josie?*' Dinah says.

I get a cold feeling. Something about Max's face, the wild expression on it... it's like he's hit some tipping point and lost control. I watch, frozen, as he closes the gap to where Josie's standing, and grips her arm. I hear the hot gasp of Dinah's breath as she lunges for the window. She batters on it, but they're too far below us and the casement's stuck fast.

And then she's out of the room, racing down the stairs, and I'm right behind her.

Chapter Nineteen
Dinah

Sunlight bursts around me. Max's voice is still going, like a hammer that can't stop. I've never seen him like this. It's like some awful dam has broken in him.

'Ruined it,' he's saying. 'You ruined it, you *made* me—'

'*Max!*' I yell.

It's like a spell breaks when he hears me. He turns, and so does Josie. I see her pale little face, round-eyed, dazed. I put out my hand for her but she stays frozen to the spot. I lock my eyes on Max.

'You need to leave,' I say. 'Now.'

He stares at me. He looks like a sleepwalker who's just waking up.

'I—' he begins, then stops.

'Josie, go inside, sweetheart,' I say, not taking my eyes from him.

He looks back at me and I see fear there, like the enormity of what's just happened is starting to dawn on him. But too late.

'You need to leave,' I say. 'And not come back.'

I feel a frozen, deadly calm. The real feelings will come later—the anger, and the grief. This is someone I loved—someone I thought I loved. I look into his eyes now and don't see that person.

'I—' He looks down at himself as if he can't figure it out either.

'You understand, don't you?' I say. I feel the pressure beating behind my eyes, the tears that won't fall. 'You can't come back. Not after this.'

'But—' He looks so lost.

I close my eyes, feeling dizzy for a moment, and when I open them Max is watching me, almost hopeful. I wait until I see it sink in on his face, until the hope is finally gone.

He opens his mouth to say something, then closes it. He shakes his head. He still looks dazed.

'I'm sorry,' he says finally, hollowly. 'I just... lost it.'

'Please,' I say. 'Just go.'

I watch him walk down the path. It's not just Max walking away. It's the future I saw, it's a piece of my faith in life.

I knew he was tightly wound, high strung. I knew he felt pressure more than other people. But there's something uncontrollable in him, I see now. Something that needs to lash out, and that aims for the weak instead of the strong.

My breath shudders out of me and I feel an arm wrap around my shoulders. Lottie holds me up and I sag into her.

Lottie shakes her head. 'That was—what got into him? Have you ever seen him like that before?'

I shake my head. What just happened wasn't about Josie, I know that much—not really. The look in

Max's eyes when he was gripping her arm... He didn't see my daughter. All he saw was his big gesture ruined. The universe sabotaging him as usual.

'I know a little about where it was coming from. I think.'

Those unguarded moments when he let slip something about his parents, about his father's intolerance for weakness. There's a hole in that boy that will never be filled, a fear of failure that runs down to his roots like a rot.

I can forgive a temper, I've been guilty of that myself. But what I can't forgive? Picking on someone not his own size. Picking on the one small human I was put on this earth to protect.

'He's gone now,' I say.

Lottie squeezes me. 'Yes. He's gone.'

And then I notice something. It's too quiet.

'Where's Josie?' I say.

Lottie glances down the garden.

'Josie?' I call. 'Jojo?'

I go around the back and call her name.

Lottie puts her head inside the kitchen door.

'Josie!' she calls.

I follow her inside, calling up the stairs. Josie's not in our room. She's not anywhere.

She's gone.

*

My hands shake on the steering wheel.

'She hasn't gone far,' Lottie says. 'She can't have.'

She glances at me. 'You used to run away from home all the time, Di,' Lottie says. 'Remember?'

I nod. I know she's saying it to help me. But Josie isn't me. Josie is a careful kid, a cautious kid, so when she does something big it means something.

And the world isn't what it was when I was her age.

This is a safe neighborhood, I remind myself.

But she's scared, in shock, alone.

I'm not someone who makes promises often—I know how hard they are to keep. But I make promises to Josie, maybe not out loud, but I make one every day. And today it feels like I've broken it.

'Josie's a really, really smart girl,' Lottie goes on. 'She won't do anything silly. You've brought her up to take care of herself, Dinah.' She looks at me. 'You're a great mother, okay?'

The words jolt something in me.

'Oh, Lottie! Your test…'

Her face tightens. I may have forgotten but she hasn't.

'Did you check it?' I ask. 'Before…?'

She shakes her head.

'You could have stayed at the house,' I say. I think about how much she loves Josie, how much she loves me, that she just jumped in the car without a second thought.

Lottie says nothing.

'You really want it to be negative, don't you?' I say.

238

She lets out a huge breath.

'I'm not like you, Di,' she says. 'You *are* a great mother. Even right at the start you were just… ready.'

I shake my head, my eyes still scanning the sidewalk. 'I just move forward, Lottie. It doesn't mean I feel sure of anything. And I wasn't "ready." I doubt anyone's "ready."'

Lottie bites her lip and says nothing. We go back to scanning the street.

'Di,' she says then. 'Do you think if you hadn't seen… if you hadn't thought it was Jeff that night… would you and he still…?'

I swallow.

'I don't think it would have worked out, Lottie. Even then. The trust was already too thin.'

The truth is, what I thought I saw that night was easy for me to believe. Easy, because it was what I'd been expecting, one way or another, for too long. Jeff wasn't a bad guy but I guess I always worried he was weak. Girls liked him, and he liked to be liked. If I'd been sure about him, I wouldn't have been up in the attic in the first place, would I? Rooting around in Mom's memory boxes for the Magic 8-Ball, in search of a cheap prophecy about whether or not Jeff and I were meant to be.

Silence falls.

'Max…' Lottie says then. 'Dinah, I've never seen someone lose control like that.'

I wince. Should I have seen the signs? Max was

always so high-strung. Never able to abide any loss of dignity. But he was so earnest. Always wanting to do the right thing. He seemed safe.

I swallow. 'There's stuff there that goes way back,' I say, remembering. 'He's told me things… about his family. About his dad. I think the pressure was insane.' One of the anecdotes comes to mind. 'Like apparently whenever he cried as a little kid, his dad would yell at him, *there's no room in this world for weakness*. What kind of a thing is that to say to a little child?'

That's when my phone suddenly starts ringing and I almost brake in the street.

'Oh my gosh. Lottie—'

She's already going through my purse for me.

'It's Vaughan,' she says quietly. And right then Lottie's phone starts ringing too.

'Mom,' she says, and I can hear the fear in her voice mirroring mine.

'Answer it!' I say.

Lottie puts it on loudspeaker.

'I'm with Dinah. What's happening?'

There's a pause. My heart batters.

The loudspeaker crackles as Mara exhales.

'Lottie. They say… they say it looks like he's doing better. A lot better.'

Something happens in my chest I don't have words for.

'His oxygen levels are still low,' Mara goes on. 'But they're climbing. They've been climbing steadily.'

I can feel the emotion radiating off Lottie.

Breathe, I remind myself. *Hope, but not too much.*

'Are they going to take him off the ventilator?' Lottie says.

'Not yet,' Mara says. 'Not yet, but hopefully soon.'

'Are you in the hospital right now?' I say.

'I'm here with your sister.' Mara's voice cracks a little. 'They said if he stays stable they'll reduce his medications and try to bring him up. They have to take him off the sedatives really slowly.'

It feels like my heart is locked against my ribs, like my breaths won't go all the way down.

'Okay.' It comes out almost a whisper.

'I'll keep you posted,' Mara says. 'We'll call you as soon as there's any news.'

'Okay,' Lottie echoes. 'Okay, Mom.'

My hands are shaking, my breath's coming fast.

'Do you want to go to the hospital?' I say when Lottie hangs up. 'You should go. I can let you out right here.'

Lottie puts her hand on my arm.

'First we'll get Josie. Then we'll go.'

And then something occurs to me and this time I do brake in the middle of the road. A car honks.

'What if she's gone to Jeff's?' I say.

'Does she know the way?'

I nod.

'Try it,' she says. I do a quick U-turn.

Lottie glances at me.

'It's going to be fine, Dinah.'

I sniff, and manage a nod.

'And Lottie?' I say. 'I just want you to know that I'll support you. Whatever happens. Whatever that test says. I just want you to know.'

Lottie gives me a tiny smile.

I swing my eyes back to the road, hang the next right. I pound the horn at the car double-parked in front of us, then swear and pull around it. The houses fly by until I swing into Jeff's street. Then Lottie grabs my arm.

'Max,' she says. 'Max is here.'

Good Lord. He's in the McCraes' driveway. He's on their doorstep. His back's to us. He's gesturing with his hands, wild and angry.

'Dinah, what's he *doing* here?'

I get out and slam the door.

'Max!'

He doesn't turn.

'You're being crazy, man.' I hear Jeff's voice. 'You're making no sense. Whatever happened between—'

'You're turning her against me,' Max shouts over him. 'I know you are.'

I see Jeff's eyes raise up over Max's head, seeing Lottie and me. He gives his head a tiny shake: *stay back.*

'Max Brannagh! I'm telling you now to get out of here!' Gillian's shouting from an upstairs window.

'I've already called your mother. And so help me, I'm calling the cops too if you don't get out of here right now.'

'Jeff,' Lottie calls, and at her voice Max turns too. The sight of us barely seems to surprise him. Whatever state he's worked himself into now, he's like a ship in full sail. How long has he been here?

'It's Josie,' I say, trying to keep my eyes away from Max. 'Jeff, have you seen her? She's—'

'You came here for him,' Max says, as if I hadn't spoken. 'I knew it.' I bet the whole neighborhood can hear. 'I knew you were lying to me.'

I can't help it; I make eye contact. And looking at his face all I can think is that he's having some kind of breakdown. Maybe that's what thirty-eight years of "not good enough" from a family like his will do to you. Nobody can walk a high-wire forever.

'Why, Dinah?' he says. 'Why couldn't I just be enough for you?'

From the corner of my eye I feel Jeff looking at me. Max takes a step my way.

'I'm telling you, this is your last warning,' Gillian shouts from upstairs.

'Dinah.' Jeff's voice cuts over the noise. 'What happened to Josie? Where is she?'

I look at Lottie. 'If she's not here, we need to go back home. One of us should be there in case she comes back-'

'God *damn* it,' Max shouts. 'Don't pretend I'm not here! Don't act like I'm nothing to you!' He's standing beside Gillian's car and now he hauls back and aims a kick at the front tire. I hear a yell from

Gillian upstairs but then something else: movement behind the car like a small animal. And then Josie edges out from behind the trunk. I hear Lottie draw a breath beside me.

'*Josie,*' I say.

She just stands there halfway down the driveway, looking at all of us.

'Josie,' I say again, and move towards her. But like a frightened animal she bolts.

'Josie!' I yell, and start to run.

She's belting down the driveway, hair flailing behind her.

'Look out!' Lottie's screaming. '*Josie!*'

'Josie!' I screech. Because suddenly there's a car speeding down the street, and Josie's running like a demon. I'm racing too and so is Lottie, two paces ahead of me. I've almost caught up when a hand pulls me back—it's Max, surging past me. And screaming down the street is the green sedan.

No, I tell the universe. *Not this. Anything but this.*

I see it happen. How the car slows but not enough. How Lottie's hand grabs Josie, wrenching her back. Lottie, off-balance, stumbling. Max arriving a moment too late.

The car horn blares. The moment freezes.

And the blaring goes on forever.

George

A voice is weeping.

George looks around him, through a darkness that's starting to lift. At least he thinks it is. For a while now he's been able to see the edges of it, a grey blur on the horizon.

Is this a forest he's in? There's chirping all around him. A strange, mechanical chirping, less like birds and more like machines. He forces his feet forward, towards the weeping. A voice he knows. A voice he's made promises to. A voice that makes the trees around him shiver.

It's Lottie, the voice is saying. *George. It's Lottie.*

Chapter Twenty
Lottie

I blink, trying to clear the grey blur from my eyes.
What happened? My head swims.

That's right. I remember now. I fell out of the
treehouse. Dinah and I were playing a game and I
fell. But it's okay, Dinah's here. She'll get Mom.
She'll make sure I'm safe.

'Lottie.' A voice says right beside me, and I blink
again.Everything's so bright, so blue.

'Lottie, are you okay?'

I squint against the brightness.

I'm not six. There is no treehouse. My sister
flickers into focus, but grown up now: forehead
creased, still just as beautiful.

'Lottie,' she chokes. 'Are you okay?'

A man's voice says something and as if by magic
I'm lifted off the ground. There's a metallic *thunk*
and I realize I'm on a platform—no, a gurney—I'm
being hoisted into—

'Wait, is this an ambulance?'

'She's back,' a man's voice says. I turn my head a
little. He's in an EMT uniform.

'You got hit by a car, miss. Can you hear me?
Please don't try to get up.'

Someone's crying. I get a last, blurry glimpse of the

world before the ambulance doors shut. Figures standing around, sun behind them. Trees. My mind struggles, searching for information.

Hit by a car.

I remember a road. Sun flashing off a car hood. Josie's hair streaming behind her.

I try to sit up.

'Josie—'

'She's fine,' Dinah says. There are tears all down her face. 'Not a scratch. She's just worried about you. We're all worried about you. You were out cold for a minute there.'

'I'm okay.' I try again to sit up. 'I don't need to be here. We just need to go home. We need to—'

'Miss? I'm just gonna ask you some questions now, okay?' It's the EMT.

'Is this necessary?' I say. 'My sister and I, we need to—'

He interrupts me.

'It's necessary. You might not feel it, but you're in shock right now. You may have injuries you're not able to feel because of the adrenalin. I'm going to ask you to please lie back down, miss.' He says it like he's not asking.

Josie's okay, I remind myself. I'm fine, she's fine…

'And Max?' I say, remembering.

Dinah nods.

'He's fine.'

He tried, I think. Despite everything, he tried.

The EMT asks his questions, and then asks me to

wiggle different fingers and toes.

'We're taking you to the ER, okay?' he says. 'You seem in pretty good shape considering, but they'll want to check you over and assess that concussion. You might have injuries I'm not able to detect right now—rib fractures, possibly.'

The hospital, I think. That's ironic.

'I called Mara,' Dinah says. 'I told her to meet us in the ER.'

I wince.

'Is she okay?'

'I told her you were coming around.' Dinah looks a little ill. 'I kind of played it down so she wouldn't freak out.'

'Thanks,' I say.

She looks down at me, puts her hand so very gently over mine. I see the horror there of what so nearly happened. And for a moment I'm back by the treehouse again: flat on my back, winded, summer sky blazing overhead; Dinah above me coming into focus. The fear on her face. The way her whole body shook with relief.

'Keep her talking,' the EMT says. 'That's the best thing for her.'

'Okay,' Dinah says, and I swear I see her jaw set just the littlest bit, like even in this situation she can't help but be a little bit anti-authoritarian, resenting being talked down to.

'"Her,"' she murmurs to me when he's not listening. 'As if you're not *right here.*'

I smile weakly. I look up at my sister and struggle to understand how we've done without each other for these past years. How we let ourselves believe that it was okay—that it was inevitable—to have drifted so very far apart. I don't remember ever fighting with Dinah as a child, despite her temper. She never raised her voice at me. That's Dinah: she'll be David against Goliath any day, but she'll never, ever hurt someone smaller or more vulnerable than her.

Which is how I know she can never, ever forgive Max for today.

'Listen,' Dinah says abruptly. 'I should tell you something. That car…'

I wait, but she stops and shakes her head.

'It'll wait,' she says. 'It's fine.'

'I'm sure someone got the registration,' I say.

She bites her lip, nods.

My mind feels jumbled. I keep seeing flashes of what happened, frozen images I can't quite thread together.

'Max ran after us, didn't he?'

Dinah nods. *But that doesn't change things,* her eyes say. It's not enough, we both know that. It could never be enough.

But there's something else. Something about Max. I don't know what it is exactly that's bothering me. It's like the blow to my head shook all these different pieces loose, like a jigsaw, and I'm scrabbling for the pieces.

Max. Something about Max. Something about—

'Dinah,' I say. She looks at me.

'What was that thing you told me earlier? About Max; about the thing his dad used to say?'

She just blinks at me.

'Lottie, are you feeling okay?'

'I'm fine,' I say, a little too loud. 'I just want you to tell me again. Something about weakness?'

She frowns.

'It was just some stupid thing from his father.'

I close my eyes, trying to remember.

'There's no room in this world for weakness,' I say. 'Right? Is that what it was?'

Dinah nods, chewing her lip.

'Are you sure you're feeling okay?'

I close my eyes again. That's it. The words on the note. 'Clyde's' words. *There's no room in this world for weakness.*

Just a phrase. Just another mean, damaging idea that gets spread around. Plenty of other people besides Max's father must have spoken it. But... Birch Bend is a small town.

Max's father. Seb Brannagh.

It slides into place.

The restaurant. I think of what Mom said, how Bonnie was always working late there.

Bonnie wasn't fired for being a bad employee. She was fired because she was having an affair with the boss. I remember then what Andrea said, what the other waitress overheard: *She stole something.*

I'm betting it was Alane who did the firing, and she wasn't talking about stolen money. It was Alane's husband Bonnie "stole." Dinah says Alane's always been so frosty with her. No *wonder*. What must Alane have thought, when she realized who Max's new girlfriend actually was?

'Lottie? Are you okay? Lottie?'

'Just wait a minute,' I say. I need to focus.

Mom said Dad didn't know who 'Clyde' was. But she was wrong, I'm sure of it now. What else would explain Dad's attitude to Max, to that whole family?

'Lottie?' Dinah says, louder this time. 'Lottie, please. Say something.'

I feel a wave of overpowering nausea, bile racing up from my stomach. I put my hand to my mouth.

'I think I'm gonna be—'

The EMT produces a bucket right in time.

*

'Oh, good *Lord*.' Mom runs over the second we're in the ER. 'Lottie, I can't believe... thank God you're all *right*.'

'I'm fine,' I say. Which I seem to be, mostly. My palms aren't even grazed because I guess I landed on my back. Things are starting to throb a little though.

'There they are!' a voice says, and I see Jeff and Josie striding our way.

'She's okay,' Dinah says, scooping Josie up. 'She's fine, Jo-bear. She's really going to be fine.'

'What about Dad?' I turn to Mom. 'How's he doing?

Is it still good?'

Mom nods, strokes my hair.

'Still good. Vaughan's with him. I told her to stay.'

'Is he awake?' I say.

'He will be,' Mom says.

'I want to see him.' They've parked my cot to the side of the ER; someone's just gone off with my paperwork. They've already had someone come along and shine a light in my eyes, ask me more questions, but I'm supposed to wait for an MRI.

Mom squeezes my hand.

'Let's wait for your MRI,' she says. 'Then we'll go.'

'I want to see him,' I say. I look at Dinah, borrowing some of her stubbornness. 'I'm fine, I know I am. I'll do the MRI after. I just want to see him first.'

'Well, they can't *make* you stay here,' Jeff says.

I nod, and scoot my legs to the side of the cot.

Dinah raises her eyebrows. 'Lottie—' she says, like I'm the rebel daughter and she's the sensible one.

'Just let me see how I feel.'

I test my weight on both arms, and lever my legs off the side of the cot. They're sturdy. The left one pulses a bit, and I know the bruising's going to be insane, but I can deal with that. Mom whistles a breath through her teeth.

'Lottie—'

'*Mom,*' I say, and she bites her lip, then nods.

We spill out of the elevator, all six of us. Yes, my left side feels a bit like someone took a baseball bat to it, but I don't think I've ever felt so strong. Mom leads the way.

And there he is.

Vaughan's sitting beside him, his hand in both of hers. Dad has his head propped up on some pillows. His eyes are open. He sees us.

Just to be seen. Just to be seen by him.

His face gives way as we come closer.

'You're all here,' he says. His words are muffled but recognizable. Josie races towards him.

'Careful!' Dinah says, and Josie brakes right at the edge of the bed. Dad reaches out a hand and pulls her close.

'My loves,' he says. 'I've missed you all so much.'

*

Jeff leaves the room at some point. The rest of us stay as long as they'll let us. There are tears, and talking in excited bursts. We take turns. We try to tamp it down so as not to overwhelm Dad. But he doesn't look overwhelmed. He looks about ten years older than he did ten days ago, but his eyes are full of gratitude and relief.

At some point when Vaughan and Mom are talking, I slip out of the room. I'm feeling overwhelmed myself all of a sudden, and I'm starting to really notice the pain now. And my brain still feels dazed, by so much of what's happened today.

Seb Brannagh and Bonnie. It feels like too big a secret to keep to myself.

And then I spot Jeff a little way down the corridor, talking to someone. I can see the tension in his back from here, but only as I walk towards them do I recognize the woman—the coiffed silver-blonde bob and sharp features. It's Alane Brannagh.

'... leave it a few days, if I were you,' Jeff is saying. 'For things to cool down.'

Then he sees me and straightens. Alane sees me too and her mouth drops open a little.

'Oh, good Lord,' she says. 'I'm just... I'm sorry, I just had to come. I had to see if you were all right.'

What's she even doing here? If anyone needs her right now, frankly, it's her son.

'I just... When I got the call from Gillian,' she goes on, 'I just jumped in the car. I was just terrified, Gillian said he was hysterical, she was on the verge of calling the police...' She shakes her head. 'I wasn't even seeing straight. And then that little girl, I almost...' Tears spring into her eyes.

My brain catches up slowly.

What Dinah began to say to me in the ambulance... it was Alane's car. Alane who almost hit Josie. Who hit *me*. I try to remember it.

'I slammed the brakes,' she says. 'As soon as I saw her. You pulled her back... you sort of spun around. You were almost clear. It was just the side of the hood that caught you, I... but you were on the ground so fast, and then you were out cold.' She looks ill. 'I just needed to know you were going to be all right...'

Jeff glances at me, apologetic, like he's failed in his role as bouncer.

'It's okay,' I say. I clear my throat. 'Actually, Jeff… could you give us a minute?'

Jeff looks between me and Alane, questioning, then nods.

When he leaves, Alane draws in a long breath. She looks like she needs propping up, like she's close to collapsing herself.

'I still can't believe it.' She looks me over like she needs to check that I'm really all right; like she's expecting blood to start pouring from my skull at any minute.

'I'm okay,' I say quietly.

She nods, and her eyes well up again.

'When I saw you there in the road, just lying there, I thought—' Her hands shake. 'I thought it was all happening again.'

'You thought what was happening again?' I say.

She closes her eyes.

'*Her*,' she whispers. 'Bonnie.'

The prickles go right down my spine.

A full-body quake goes through Alane. For a moment I think she's about to be sick.

'It was unforgivable,' she says. 'I've never forgiven myself for what happened. Never.'

The air feels dry in my throat. Drier and drier.

'Bonnie died in an accident,' I say slowly. 'Didn't she?'

'Of course it was an accident. But…' Alane shakes

her head. 'I told your father I was ready to face the consequences, you know. I told him he could call the police, I was ready for it. But he said no. He said he didn't want to rake any more mud over his wife's legacy.'

There's a silence then. I feel the hospital around us, its noises. It all seems unreal.

'I know about the affair,' I say. 'But I'd like you to tell me exactly what happened that night. The accident.'

Alane draws another shuddering breath, nods.

'I was… I was a mess when I found out about it. I'd called her into the office and fired her on the spot. They both swore it had been over for weeks.' She looks down. 'And I thought that was the end of it. But then a few days later I left the restaurant early—I wasn't feeling well, I had this blinding migraine—and as I was driving up to the house I saw her car pulling out.' She stops. '*My* house. She'd come to my house, where my family was. Where I was raising my child.' Alane looks at me, a shred of desperation in her face. 'The pictures started running through my head again: the two of them together, whispering, laughing about me. In my home, *our* home.'

I feel frozen in place as she goes on.

'Her car was already pulling out of our driveway. She didn't see me turn and follow. I don't know what I thought would happen: if she'd stop and get out; if I was picturing some knock-down fight in the middle of the street. I honestly don't know. But I just couldn't take my foot off the gas. And she must have seen me then. She sped up, and I... I felt she was *taunting* me. We were both going so fast. She took those turns like...' Alane shakes her head. 'And I saw her charge down that road, right past the sign, and I just followed.

'And then I saw her car swerve off the road. I saw it all in my headlights.' She stops. 'I knew I had to see if she was... if she was all right. I got out of my car and climbed down the bank to get to her but she was...' Alane meets my eyes. 'She was gone.'

She looks away.

'And what I did next was the worst part. I got back in the car and drove home. At some point I called in a tip to the police but I didn't give a name. I didn't say a word to anyone about it.' She sniffs. 'I knew at the time that it was wrong. But... Max was only four. He needed me. He'd done nothing wrong. I didn't know what might happen to me, what I might be accused of. If everything about the affair came out they would think I'd meant for it to happen, or worse. I didn't know if I'd end up in jail, or....'

She trails off. I stare at her, trying to absorb it all.

What she did—running away like that, instead of staying and calling an ambulance right there—it was horribly wrong, but I can't pretend it wasn't in some way understandable. That it wasn't *human*.

Alane's breathing fast, her bony chest going up and down.

'And my father…' I hesitate. 'He knows all this?'

Alane fixes those pain-filled eyes on me.

'I didn't mean for him to know. I figured I'd take it to my grave. But the next week Seb brought in my car to George's garage. The tar had gotten all up in my tire treads. Not that I'd realized. I hadn't been able to bring myself to even sit in the car since that night. But Seb had noticed. He drove it into the garage. When I realized it, I was sure George would make the connection. He'd seen Bonnie's car, after all, he'd have seen those tires on her car. And the cops had probably told him about the anonymous call.'

She kneads her hands together.

'I went to pick up the car and face him.' Alane exhales. 'He'd known about the affair. I told him everything about that night, I told him to tell the police if he wanted. Only a week had gone by, but I was already starting to think it would be a relief, just to tell the truth after all.' She looks at me. 'But it would all have come out then, about the affair, about everything. He said he didn't want to do that to Bonnie or his daughters. He just looked at me with this… this deep hatred, and told me to tell no one.'

She looks at me.

'So I didn't.'

Until now.

'I just want you to know, not a day goes by that I don't remember.' She looks at me. 'I know that it's nothing compared to what your father or your sisters have all had to live with.'

I nod slowly.

'It was like some cruel joke,' she says. 'When Max chose Dinah. Out of all the girls he could have asked out... She looks so *like* Bonnie.' Alane swallows. 'I guess he has his father's taste.'

We're silent for a moment then. I feel my breath go in, and go out.

'Dinah isn't going to marry Max,' I say to her. 'Not after today. You know that, right?'

She looks down at her hands.

'I know.'

Something else occurs to me. 'So, why *was* Bonnie at your house that night? If the affair was over?'

Alane sighs.

'Seb told me about it, much later. He said Bonnie had been worried about her family. About the gossip. The effect it might have on her daughters, if rumors started going around. She came to ask Seb to ask *me* not to... well, not to drive the knife in, I suppose. The Brannaghs have always been a powerful family around here. She knew how furious I'd been. I suppose she was starting to worry about the consequences.'

I wonder if she hears the horrible irony there that I do. *The consequences.* If Bonnie hadn't driven to the Brannaghs' house that night, the consequences would have been so different...

'The thing is, you know,' Alane speaks again. Her voice is different now, dreamier, like she's off in another world. 'The thing is, I wasn't brought up to just be "somebody's wife." My parents were wonderful people, ahead of their time. Others might've been disappointed to have only one daughter, but they gave me everything. I was the first in the family to go to college. They raised me for independence. I even had a dream of going into medicine.' She swallows. 'But then I met Seb, and I did everything I'd been raised not to do. I put my own dreams back in a box and became somebody's wife. His family owned the restaurant so I became, well, a slave to that.' She looks away. 'Seb did the fun stuff while I sat in the back office and crunched numbers and tried to hold the whole miserable show together. I spent my days pleasing *his* mother, running *his* business, raising his child. And look where it got me.' She stops.

'I was so *furious* that night. When I saw her car in the driveway it was like something erupted in me. It was only later I realized it wasn't really at Bonnie. It wasn't even Seb I was so angry at. It was at myself.'

She looks over at me then.

I nod. I can't say *it's okay* or *I understand,* but I nod.

She clears her throat.

'I want you to know,' she says. 'You should do whatever you want about today. I'd write you a check right now, but you should probably sleep on it first. I'll pay whatever you decide is fair. Of if you want to sue, sue. Do what's best.' She spreads her hands. 'It's up to you.'

I nod again. Then I glance back down the corridor, where my family is.

My family.

'I have to go,' I say to Alane.

*

The doctor says it's maximum two people in the room with Dad, and only for another ten minutes: we've already "tired him out" enough for the day. Vaughan and I decide to leave Mom and Dinah for now.

'Did I see you earlier,' Vaughan says as we leave, 'talking with Alane Brannagh?'

'It's a long story,' I say.

Vaughan looks at me quizzically, but doesn't push it.

I don't know if Dad made the right decision to keep Bonnie's secret. Maybe. And is it still the right decision, all these years later? I don't know. Part of me thinks my sisters should know the truth. Part of me says, *to what purpose?* After all, the truth is only what we make of it. When the worst of this is behind us, I'll talk to Dad about it all. In the end it's his secret to tell.

Just like I have mine.

I look at Vaughan again, walking beside me. And then I feel something in my body. Not the throbbing of my muscles. Not the sickness I felt earlier.

I swallow. 'Vaughan? Where are the restrooms?'

She points. 'Are you okay?'

'Yeah,' I say. My voice sounds shrill. 'Fine.'

The restroom is cool and empty. My hands are trembling. I go into a stall and lock the door.

It's here.

I'm not pregnant.

I close my eyes.

So *was* I just late? Or… was it something more?

I lean against the wall of the bathroom stall, wanting to cry with relief and yet feeling guilty.

I think of that little stick on the attic window ledge back home. It knows the answer. But I guess it doesn't matter now. I feel a wave of guilt again and take a deep breath. Someday I'll be ready. And that day will be a good day.

I sit in the stall and cry a little longer. I'm crying because Dad's back, and I'm crying about the tiny whisper of life that might have been here and now is not, and which I absolutely didn't want but feel a need to bear witness to, if it really was here. I can't tell which tears are sad ones and which are relief. And then I find myself crying for the Lottie of long ago, and for Dinah, and the children we were and the ways those children got hurt.

Maybe this was the problem in the end for Dinah and me: we didn't know how to fight. We didn't have the training for it, and we didn't know what to do when it happened. Mom and Dad never fought—with each other or anyone else—and when Dinah yelled and acted out as a kid, their disappointment sat over all of us like a fog for days, and all we moved around inside it like frightened inhabitants of the same small island, unable to find each other though we were standing so close. Dinah was just a small, hurt child. Did they think her helpless anger was so dangerous?

I wonder if that was how we were taught to think—*if you sense conflict, build a wall.* And if Mom and Dad unknowingly taught us that, then who taught *them*?

But we have time, I tell myself, blowing my nose and wiping my face. The past is past, and we all still have time. *That* is today's greatest gift.

Vaughan walks into the bathroom as I'm washing my hands.

'I just wanted to check on you,' she says. 'I was worried you were going to faint or something. Are you feeling all right?'

I nod.

We stand there a moment, and then she pulls me into a hug.

'I love you so much, Lottie,' she says.

I flush. We don't really say things like that in our family.

'I love you too.'

She sniffs and pulls back. 'I can't believe the day we've all been through. Come on,' she says. 'Let's get you back for that MRI.'

We walk down the corridors. Jeff's taken Josie to the cafeteria to wait.

'Are you sure you're okay?' she says. 'I know it's been a hell of a day. It's just... you looked like you had something big on your mind.'

I look at her, so caring and competent. Watching me with those calm, silver eyes.

I realize there'll never be a good time. But there'll never be a better time. It's not up to me to decide what she does with the truth. It's just up to me to speak it.

'Vaughan,' I say. 'There's something I should have told you long ago. I should have told you then, but I think I still have to tell you. Even though it's in the past. And even though you'll hate hearing it.'

And hate me, maybe.

'Before I do,' I say. 'I just want you to know I'm sorry.'

She looks at me. I don't know what she hears in my voice exactly, but she hears enough. She takes a breath. Looks at me with her calm, brave eyes.

'Okay,' she says. 'Tell me.'

Chapter Twenty-one
Dinah

The nurse finishes changing the drip.

'Okay, you two.' He looks at Mara and me. 'Five more minutes.'

'Thank you,' Dad says.

Dad's eyes are bright. Clear. He looks tired and ill but he looks like *himself*. I realize only now how much I doubted this moment would ever happen.

'Dinah,' he beckons me, the IV needle still in his arm. I guess I've been hanging back a bit, with all the others in the room. My heart's gone places in the last ten days I never dreamed it would. Now Dad squeezes my hand and my eyes meet his, and it's like everything lifts from me in a rush, so fast I feel unsteady. I burst into messy, shuddering tears that I don't even try to stop. I don't know how long it lasts—maybe less than a minute but it feels like hours—but when I come back to myself Mara's stroking my back. Mara, of all people.

I hiccup. She puts her hand on my shoulder.

'Oh, sweetheart.' That's not a word she's used for me before. 'Why don't I leave you two alone for a minute. I'll see you first thing tomorrow,' she says, and puts her hand to Dad's face.

The door closes and Dad and I sit in silence. There's a box of tissues by his bed, and he nudges them towards me.

'Better out than in,' he says. A George Spencer classic.

I take one.

'Daddy?' I say. I hesitate. But I need to ask.

' I... we found your email,' I say. 'To Matty Atkins.'

His face veils over and he closes his eyes. I feel the tiredness in him now.

'Matty was right,' he sighs. 'I should have talked to you first. But I was in a bad way over it all. Alane came by the shop, told me Max was going to ask you—'

'*Alane*?' I say. I can't picture it, her coming to find Dad with the news. Why would she? They barely know each other.

Dad looks at me. 'She had her reasons, Dinah.'

'But you barely know her.'

Dad closes his eyes.

'There are some things I've never told you, Dinah. About Alane. That family.' He blinks. 'It just never occurred to me that you and Max, you know...' He stops. 'But I suppose Mara was right. You're a grown woman, and I need to respect your choices.'

'Dad,' I say. 'I'm not going to marry Max.'

He's silent. I can feel him searching my face, not sure if I'm sure.

'I'm not,' I say again.

He searches my face a moment longer, and I guess he sees the finality there.

'As for the will.' He looks away. 'I was going to talk to you about it. I knew you'd be angry. But Matty said a trust was the only way to protect you.'

I frown.

'What trust?'

Dad looks at me. 'Matty called it a blood trust. He said it would protect your inheritance from Max. So if, you know, you divorced or anything, he wouldn't have any claim on it. Or if, God forbid, something happened to you, it would go straight to Josie.' He sighs. 'I knew it was a betrayal of your intentions. But I just couldn't bear a Brannagh having control of your mother's house...'

I bite my lip.

'But your email didn't say anything about a trust. It just said Vaughan and Lottie would have care of the house…'

Dad frowns.

'Not the *house*. Care of the *trust*. Someone would have to administer it after I was gone. Matty said it should be an outsider, someone who wasn't part of the family. He said making siblings administrators for each other led to in-fighting and resentments. But I was sure you three would figure it out.'

I close my eyes.

'Oh, my dear.' Dad folds a hand over mine. 'How did you think I'd have written you out of that house? You're the one who loves it the most.'

I shake my head, then start nodding. I guess I'd be crying again if I weren't all cried out. I look at the pile of crumpled tissues in my lap.

'The thing is... I know I was never the "easy" daughter,' I say. 'But I never wanted to be the black sheep.'

'Dinah,' he says. 'You're not a black sheep.'

I don't meet his eyes.

'Maybe not a black sheep, then,' I say. 'Just not one of your silver girls.'

'Oh, Dinah.' He shakes his head, something between tender and exasperated. 'Don't you know why I call your sisters that?'

I sniff. 'It's from the song,' I say. 'The Simon and Garfunkel one. You used to play it for Lottie all the time.'

Dad sighs.

'No, the song came later. You don't remember the poem, Dinah? That Yeats one your mother loved?'

I shake my head. 'I didn't know Mom liked Yeats.'

He looks abashed.

'I sometimes forget how young you were. Vaughan remembers.' He smiles a little. 'Your mother *loved* Yeats. She used to recite that one to you two at bedtime.'

He looks at me, clears his throat:

'*I'll walk among long dappled grass,*
And pluck till time and times are done,
The silver apples of the moon,
The golden apples of the sun.'

He stops. 'Silver for the moon, gold for the sun. You were always our little fireball.'

He shakes his head and puts his hand on mine.

'Don't you know, Dinah, you're my golden apple?'

I guess I'm not all cried out after all.

Three weeks later

There are no caterers for the party this time. No rented chairs, no silverware, no tablecloths. No guests. We just pull our old, battered kitchen table out onto the back lawn and we order pizza, and we eat out there as the July evening ebbs around us. Dad's taken out the nicest bottle of wine he owns, one a client gave him a few Christmases ago and he's been saving. He's sticking to seltzer, but the rest of us are savoring it.

Josie snuggles into my lap as the sun goes down. I lift my nice full glass and take a swallow, then burrow my nose in Josie's hair and plant a kiss on her scalp.

'Mommy!' she protests.

'Sorry, baby,' I say, and she sighs but leans back into me anyway.

I look down the table: Dad and Mara; my two sisters. Lottie's glowing, but Vaughan still looks pale and worn. Mitchell drove up from Connecticut the day after they let Dad out of the hospital, and picked her up. I watched from the front window as he got out of the car and slowly walked up the driveway. Mitchell's always been one of those people who acted like the world's a buffet and they got first plate. But watching him walk up the driveway towards Vaughan, I felt sorry for him. I almost admired him,

270

even. I could see how every step was bringing him pain but he didn't shirk it.

She didn't move to greet him. She just stood there as he took her bags, and then walked ahead of him to the car. If words were spoken, I didn't hear them.

He does love her. I believe that. I think he loves her a lot.

But I wasn't surprised when she rang a few days later to tell me that it was over.

Meanwhile, I've been trying to strike the right balance with Josie, telling her things about Max, about what happened, about why I'm not getting married any more. I didn't want to make her feel guilty thinking I didn't marry him because of what happened with her. I never wanted her to imagine it was her 'fault.' She seems worried, though, about me being alone.

'Mommy, are we a family?' she'd said, sitting on her bed, spinning Pig's legs into an uncomfortable looking configuration.

'Of course we are.' I tilted her chin up to look at me. 'You're worried that we're not a family? Because I'm not with Max anymore?'

'But...' She danced Pig across her lap and sat him down. 'But are you still going to be happy, if it's just me?'

I had to swallow really hard then. I pulled her into my lap, tight enough that she squealed. I put on my most serious voice.

'Josie. You make me happier than anyone else in

the world, you know that?'

She nodded.

'But it's too much pressure for you to be the *only* thing that makes me happy. So never feel like my happiness depends on just you, okay? Because it doesn't.'

She nodded, very slowly. I wanted to drive the point home, to be sure as sure could be that she'd absorbed the message. But this isn't a conversation you have in one go, I realized. It's one that you have again and again, as many times as it takes. True love doesn't ask for quick fixes, and Josie is my one true love.

'But who will take care of you,' she'd said then, frowning, 'if you don't have Max or Daddy?'

I guess I could have used it as a feminist moment, and told her women didn't *need* to be taken care of. But Josie's a pure soul, one who still believes in a model for humanity where everyone, woman or man, can rest easy in the knowledge they're cared for, and watched over.

'I have lots of people to take care of me,' I told her. 'But *you* don't need to take care of me, baby, that's not your job.'

Her face was still skeptical.

'*I* take care of me, and Grandpa takes care of me. And Mara,' I added, feeling generous. 'And my friends. And my sisters.'

Odd, it was at the word *sisters* that I could tell she believed me.

She looked at me with that funny, pensive look she gets sometimes.

'I wouldn't mind having a sister one day.'

'I'll bear that in mind,' I said, careful to keep a straight face.

I'm called back to the moment by the gentle *ding ding ding* of a knife on a glass, and Mara clears her throat.

We all look her way and it's dusk so I'm not sure, but I think she blushes. I don't ever remember seeing Mara blush, strange as that sounds. Something has changed in her these past weeks. If I were being unkind—which I'm trying not to be these days—I could say that the Ice Queen was melting. There's a pinkness in her cheeks that didn't used to be there, I'm sure of it. She laughs differently; she curses while driving; I even heard her singing along to the radio the other day in the kitchen. I don't know how to describe it except to say that she seems younger by about ten years.

'I just want to say,' she clears her throat again, 'I guess I just want to say that I'm grateful. For—' her voice breaks, and I look down at my glass. 'For *life*'—she gives Daddy a look so fierce it could catch fire, then her gaze pans around the rest of us—'and for all of those who make it worth living.' She sniffs a bit, in a remarkably undignified way, considering it's Mara.

'To my family,' she says.

'To family,' we all say, and Josie shifts on my lap to

look around at me.

Now, Lottie clears the remainders of pizza off the table and announces that she's baked a key lime pie for dessert. Josie drums her silverware on the table until I tickle her into stopping.

Lottie never did look at that pregnancy test. She asked me the day we got home from the hospital if I would mind just bagging it up and throwing it away. She didn't want to know what it said. I figured I wouldn't be able to hide the answer if I knew, so I didn't look either as I scooped it into the trash.

She'll make a great mother someday, if she wants to.

She's told me a bit about the guy. And although she hasn't told me, I've inferred from the way her phone keeps buzzing these days that they might be talking again. Which is nice, I think. He sounds good for her.

I glance across the table at my other sister, her arm stretched easily around Dad's wide frame as he looks up at the summer stars. Vaughan's going back to Connecticut on Monday, but we've promised each other that tomorrow we'll all sit down and talk through what Daddy and Mara need, and make a plan. It's going to be a bit-by-bit road to recovery, but we'll take it one step at a time.

As for Vaughan, would she have ended things with Mitchell if it hadn't been for Lottie's story? I don't know. Maybe it's hard to know what you're prepared to live with until you get there. But

Vaughan seems to be doing a little better each day.

I want her to be happy, so happy. She deserves it.

Daddy's finally told us all what he was going to say that day of the party—the big throat-clearing speech he was about to make. It was a retirement announcement. Which honestly *did* come as a surprise, after all that. Mara had been nudging him to retire for years, but he'd never wanted to. But apparently he'd been thinking about it over the last six months, realizing he wasn't getting any younger, and Mara had always talked about how much she wanted to see France one day. Dad's big idea was to rent a cottage there for a few months and hit retirement with a bang. He figured they'd get a lodger in   while they were away to help with bills and Lottie could still live there if she wanted to. Overall it was a surprisingly romantic, somewhat impractical plan that he'd meant to unveil to Mara that night with everybody present—a proposal, I guess you could say.

'So what *are* you going to do?' Lottie says, over a forkful of the key lime pie. 'Instead of France?'

Because although I hope they'll get to travel to France one of these days, nobody's letting Dad get on an airplane anytime soon.

'Cooking,' Dad says promptly. 'I've decided if I can't take your mother to France, I'll take France to her. I'm going to start classes. And I'm going to make her the best damn *boeuf bourguignon* she's ever tasted.'

Mara laughs, and so do the rest of us. Dad looks so pleased with himself, almost mischievous.

'Really?' Lottie says. Dad's never been exactly famous for his culinary skills.

'Yes. Really,' he says, sounding a little aggrieved.

'Don't forget the *creme brulée*,' Vaughan adds, smiling.

'So demanding,' Dad mock-grumbles. 'Aren't they, Josie?'

Josie nods back soberly.

'I'll clear the table,' I say, when everyone's made the most of desert. Josie slides off my lap, complaining.

'Well, help me then,' I say, and together we clear the plates and stack them, and carry them back into the kitchen. She hovers while I fill the dishwasher.

'What's this?' she says.

I turn around. She's picked up the Magic 8-Ball I brought down from the attic earlier. I just decided I wanted to have it. Something superstitious, I guess.

So here's a thought experiment: if I'd been *sure* about Max, absolutely sure, would I have gone up into the attic that day in search of Mom's old novelty-store fortune-teller?

And if I hadn't gone up there, and found Lottie in such a state, would she and I have ever really tackled the past?

And if instead I'd been downstairs, or out in the garden with Josie… if I'd been the one to see Max first, if he hadn't startled Josie with her soccer ball…

So maybe it's better not to know too much about what's next?

Take that, Magic 8-Ball.

'Well?' Josie says impatiently, jiggling the ball in her two hands.

'It's supposed to help you answer questions about the future,' I say, and smile when her eyes widen.

'But it's a toy,' I add. 'It's not real.'

She huffs. 'Then what's the point?'

'Well.' I pause. 'I think sometimes we might know the answer to things, but we just need a little help knowing how we really feel.'

I see her weighing up the response. She looks away, and rolls the ball back and forth on the counter.

'Or maybe it's a *little* bit magic,' she says finally.

I laugh.

'Maybe.'

Maybe a lot of things are.

'Aunt Lottie showed me a doll of Grandma's upstairs,' she says then. 'She says I can have it if I want.'

'Do you?' I say.

'I don't know,' Josie muses. 'I think maybe I'm a little old for dolls. But I like that one. It kind of looks like me.'

I know the one she's talking about. It does look just like her. Like Mom.

I had a talk with Vaughan yesterday, about Mom. The kind of talk we never have, and probably should have had a lot more of over the years. I asked her if she still misses Mom and she said not really. She thinks about her a lot, but she doesn't exactly miss her.

Is it weird that that I still really miss her? I said. Because I do. A lot, sometimes. Even though I barely knew her.

Vaughan shook her head.

Of course not. But—and don't take this the wrong way, Di—you might also be missing the perfect version of her.

I got the sense she meant something particular by that, but when I asked she hesitated. She said she'd picked up things over the years about Mom and Dad's marriage. About Mom being… erratic. Kind of unreliable. A little reckless. She looked at me.

You don't remember the fighting, do you?

I just remember that I loved her so much, I said.

Vaughan nodded. *She was just like a kid. I think we loved that about her.*

Mara breezes into the kitchen, carrying the empty bottle of wine.

'I think we should open some champagne,' she says. 'I know we have some here somewhere.'

'Pushing the boat out, Mara,' I grin.

She stops and looks at me. Maybe I sounded sarcastic when I said that—I didn't mean to. I guess sometimes I come off fiercer than I intend. I never feel all that tough on the inside.

Mara looks back at me.

'Dinah?'

I brace myself. *Whatever it is, don't get into it tonight, Dinah. Tonight is a good night.*

'Yes?' I say.

Mara clears her throat. Then she draws me into the awkwardest side-hug I've ever experienced.

'I—I just want you to know that I love you.'

She looks at me. I try and smile, but my face doesn't quite know what to do.

'Sorry I haven't said that before,' she says.

Very cautiously, like we're both made of glass, I slowly put my arms around her.

Nothing bad happens.

I exhale.

This could almost feel… normal. One day.

'Me too, Mara,' I say. Because I think probably, deep down, despite everything, it might be true.

There's a thump from the kitchen counter as Josie drops the 8-Ball. I release Mara and clear my throat. It's going to take a lot more tries before that hug becomes a habit.

'Sorry!' Josie peers over the ball to read the floating message.

'So what does it say, Jojo?' I ask.

She looks up at me and smiles. Outside, I hear Dad laughing with Vaughan and Lottie, their voices bright against his like moonlight, like silver bells.

Josie holds up the ball.

'Signs point to yes,' she says.

Epilogue
Sixteen months later

George Spencer is looking at the Christmas tree when the phone rings. He hears Mara pick up and goes back to trying to decide whether the tree is straight. He'll check with her once she's off the phone, she's always had a better eye for these things.

But he doesn't get to check, because suddenly she's yelling his name from the hallway.

'George! Hurry! The hospital!'

His heart speeds up. He goes quickly to the kitchen doorway and looks in. Mara's already grabbing her purse from the counter, scrabbling for car keys.

'Was that...?'

Mara nods.

George grabs his coat, and without even turning off the lights or setting the alarm, they race to the car.

*

Something clunks in the back seat as Mara pulls onto the highway. George glances over his shoulder. It's that 8-Ball toy that Josie's always playing with whenever she's at their place.

Mara accelerates, and the ball tumbles back against the seat.

'Are the others…?'

Mara nods, her hands tight on the wheel. 'They're there.'

George closes his eyes, thinking once more about the unexpected turns life has taken since his brush with mortality last year.

Dinah, for starters. She told him something the other day on the phone that's stuck with him. She said that learning how to love a widower was making her a better person, a more generous person. *But it's hard sometimes, too.* She'd paused. *Mara must have had to be very strong.*

She was, George had said. *She is.*

He would have thought Dinah and Jeff would be the couple who were always fighting, but it doesn't seem to be that way after all. *Maybe Dinah's losing her edge,* he'd said to Mara recently, but she just smiled.

Lottie and Roman, meanwhile, seem to spar all the time, which is a surprise too. Lottie, his most conciliatory daughter. But George is happy about that. It's good for her. She's learning how to fight, he thinks: how to push and still be safe. Roman seems to energize her in a way that's new. She's changing.

It amazes him how they're all still changing, even after so much time.

Mara swings onto the exit ramp, and soon they're lurching over the speed bumps into the hospital complex.

They're looking for the maternity unit.

Funny the way things work out.

It broke George's heart more than a little to see Vaughan's marriage dissolve, but she was really quite strong about it, remarkably philosophical in the end. Sometimes people really do have irreconcilable differences. Then when she told them that she was planning to have a baby on her own, at first George was pretty doubtful. He tried to make the right noises—he didn't want to offend her—but he couldn't help thinking it was rash and that she'd regret it later, not waiting. But he kept his skeptical moments to himself, and he has to admit, these last few months she's never looked happier.

Josie, meanwhile, has all sorts of thoughts about what the baby should be called. Like most recently, if it's a girl: Magnolia.

He looks over at Mara as she jerks up the emergency brake and takes the keys from the ignition.

'Ready?' she says.

'Ready.' He smiles.

*

When they're finally allowed able to go in and see her, he's first through the door. Everyone's hushed, even Josie, who until now had been bouncing with excitement.

'Everyone,' Vaughan says, and tweaks the tiny striped cap on the tiny, wrinkled head. 'Meet George Junior. George Junior, meet your family.'

She lets them hold him, one by one.

George finds it hard to release his brand-new

grandson into Mara's arms. His cheeks feel damp when he finally does.

'Dad.' He gets a dig in the ribs from Dinah.'Get it together,' she grins. 'You're embarrassing us.'

He elbows her back, weakly.

'You're a dreadful brat, you know that?' George wipes the tears from his face and grins back at her.

'Hey! You two!' Someone chides. 'You'll wake the baby.'

Baby George snuffles in Mara's arms and they all stare as he opens his eyes, closes them, opens them again.

George catches Josie looking around at the adults. She seems nonplussed.

'Your little cousin doesn't do much, does he?' George grins. 'But you just wait.'

When it's time for Vaughan to try nursing, he and Mara head out to give her some privacy.

'Anything we can get you?'

'I'd kill for a bagel,' Vaughan says. 'The food in this place is plain awful.'

'Josie,' Mara turns. 'Want to come with us? We can get ice cream.'

'Yes!' Josie brightens.

Outside in the doorway George pauses a moment, looking back through the glass panel. His three daughters are framed there like a triptych. Two blonde heads, one dark.

'My girls,' he sighs. He doesn't think hearts get much fuller than this.

Mara nudges him. '*Our* girls,' she says, and puts an arm around his back.

And George hears a third voice too—a voice he still catches, very faintly, on days when the mood is right.

Our girls, Bonnie's voice echoes, and George hears the smile in it.

Our beautiful, beautiful girls.

THE END

A Letter from Claire

Thank you so much, dear reader, for spending your time with me, and with the characters of *The First Wife's Secret*. I'm honored that you chose to spend some of your precious leisure hours here. I hope you enjoyed the read!

I absolutely loved writing my first book, *The Silent Daughter*, but writing this second book was a new, incredible journey. If you've been with me since *The Silent Daughter* you'll probably agree that *The First Wife's Secret* is a little different: more of an emotional drama this time than a thriller, though hopefully still a twisty read that kept you guessing. Death and danger loom in *The First Wife's Secret* too, but the biggest danger is one I'm sure we all fear most: the prospect of losing someone we love.

If you've read *The Silent Daughter*, maybe you'll spot some common themes in *The First Wife's Secret*: the pull of the past, and the many ways we can find ourselves "haunted"; the difficult decisions we make about what to believe, whom to trust, and what kind of people we want to be in the world.

I read Daphne du Maurier's novel *Rebecca* when I was 13 or thereabouts, and I remember being absolutely spellbound by it. It popped back into my mind as I was writing *The First Wife's Secret*. (I guess *The First Wife's Secret* could have been a very apt title for *Rebecca* too, come to think of it!) The unnamed narrator of *Rebecca,* of course, is a second wife who lives in the shadow of the deceased first wife, Rebecca. Rebecca's ghost becomes so overpowering that the second wife feels almost suffocated by her. Whether the "ghost" is anything more than the narrator's imagination is in the end up to the reader, but I think du Maurier's amazing novel is a perfect dramatization of how the past can sometimes overpower us, and how complicated our relationships to "ghosts" can be, even if the ghosts are of our own making.

When Dinah and Josie go to look at a brand new house and Dinah explains to her daughter that no one has ever lived there before, it's a startling thought. A *new* house? No history? No ghosts?

The thing is, we can achieve that with houses—we *can* be "the first". But when it comes to people, no one we meet is a blank canvas. (Except for newborns, possibly!) As adults, we build relationships with other people knowing that everyone carries their own set of memories, and maybe a ghost or two.

Being the "first" anything can be challenging, but it is often a position of power. *I was here first,* we say, even as kids, arguing over who has more right to be here, or a bigger claim on the prize. *First* becomes a kind of trophy. In so much of our lives—maybe more so than ever in our modern world, where social media seems to automatically compare us to everyone else we know—we are prone to feeling ranked. Who is first? Who is second? Who is last? Who has earned their place and who has not?

First can sometimes seem to have too much power, shaping the story in advance for those who join it later. And of course this isn't just about first and second spouses—how often do we hear of second siblings feeling constricted by a particular set of expectations, feeling the pressure of coming second? Often, the most potent "ghosts" are the people that used to stand where we're standing; the ones who were once in our shoes and whether they meant to or not, left patterns in their wake that we have to grapple with.

So what does it mean to be a "first" wife, or a "first" anything? A lot of *The First Wife's Secret* is about learning to untangle those rivalries—rivalries we're not always aware we're playing into. Lottie Spencer wonders if her mother was loved as much as her dad's first wife, and what that says about her family if not. Meanwhile Dinah carries old resentments about her stepmother, "the second wife"; Dinah also has hang-ups of her own about being the "second" daughter and how she measure up to older sister Vaughan. Of course, in the end Dinah effectively becomes a "second wife" herself, as she reconnects with a man who has lost a previous love. Dinah comes to accept that living with someone else means living with their ghosts, and that this doesn't have to be a bad thing. Sometimes complexity helps us grow.

Ultimately, both Lottie and Dinah learn to accommodate the "ghosts" in their lives. As Roman points out to Lottie, ghosts are defined by absence, but it's our presence that makes life worth living. I think both Lottie and Dinah, by the end of the story, are more fully present in their own lives than they were at the start.

So what is the first wife's "secret" in the end? On a basic level of course it's the fact of the affair. But at another level, maybe the secret is that nobody's as perfect as we imagine, or is living as idyllic a life as we've been led to believe. And maybe it's being a little less than perfect which connects us to each other…

I hope you've enjoyed making some new connections as you read *The First Wife's Secret*. If you'd like to stay in touch, I'd be delighted! My website is claireamarti.com, and you can find me on Facebook at facebook.com/claireamartiauthor, or follow me on Amazon or Bookbub. You'll also find links to sign up to my monthly Reading Group newsletter on my website, if you're interested.

Finally, if I could ask you a great favor: if you've enjoyed the book and if you have time, would you consider leaving a review on Amazon, or on whatever platform you share your thoughts? Reviews are everything, especially for a relatively new writer. They help other readers discover something new, and maybe even take a chance investing some of *their* precious leisure hours in a new read!

Thanks again, dear reader, for making it this far. It means the world to me that you came along for the ride with the Spencer family and their rollercoaster of a journey! I loved sharing it with you.

Take care,
Claire

Acknowledgments

First off, a huge, huge thanks to my readers. A year ago, before my first book published, I wasn't sure if I'd have *any* readers, except for my stalwart champions of friends and family! But in the almost-year since then it's been the most joyful and humbling experience, hearing from you all— real-live people, taking time out from your real-live lives to drop a line! I've loved hearing from each of you—your feedback on what you enjoyed or what ideas or characters you related to. I've loved hearing the little details you've shared about your own lives and how your experiences made you feel connected to the story. It's amazing the way a made-up story can somehow start to feel true when it resonates with someone far away, through whatever coincidences of fate.

Thank you for sharing those little gems with me. Thank you for sharing my work with your friends, for leaving reviews, and everything else that helped put a little grease under these new-writer wheels. Without it, there might not be a second book, and I'm so glad there is!

Of course, in some ways writing a second book was harder than the first. Now that I *had* readers, I had to worry about disappointing them, or not delivering a second book fast enough! So the past few months, my friends and family have had to put up with a somewhat more antisocial version of me, who spent too much time chained to her desk, and didn't always get quite enough sleep!

Thanks to my dear friends for seeming to still remember who I am despite my AWOL months. Thanks once again Margaret Gales for keeping my head in the game and for proofreading better than the pros!; to RFG and NKB for all the support and insight; to the Dumplings and the (misleadingly named!) "Dentures" gang (including Alma Kelliher for subtitle input when I couldn't think straight!) for all their help in getting this clunky rocket to launch. You also gave me some good laughs when I needed them; I am very grateful for those Whatsapp chats. Thanks to cousins, aunts and uncles for being such a supportive tribe—it means so much.

Very special thanks to CJ Holm for the smiling support and steady encouragement, always magically delivered in a way that didn't make me scowl with skepticism.

Big thanks to Manuel Dudli Bertrán—I look forward to raising a glass of bubbly with you soon! Thank you for taking such pride in me—it makes me very proud! Special thanks to one of New York's Finest, Dr Franklin C Lowe of Montefiore Medical Center. If there are medical inaccuracies in this book, he is innocent of them! And while his medical expertise was valuable, the support was *in*valuable. Thank you.

Thank you to my marvelous parents. You are just the bees' knees. My love of reading, writing, and that barely curbable instinct to peer into all the lighted windows—it all comes from somewhere! Thank you for instilling and nurturing all that's good and joyful in my life.

Finally—this book is dedicated to my grandparents. They're not around to see it, but they're not *not* here. Writing this story made me think a lot about legacies—about which parts of us travel down the line, through our genes, our actions, and our stories—and about how we don't have to be perfect to leave great riches in our wake. And perhaps—as some might say—we're "as near perfect as makes no difference"!